MOONLIGHT & MAGIC

MYSTERIES OF MOONLIGHT MANOR
BOOK 2

MOLLY FITZ

TRIXIE SILVERTALE

Copyright © 2022 by Molly Fitz & Trixie Silvertale.

All rights reserved. Except as permitted under the U.S. Copyright Act of 1976, no part of this publication may be reproduced, distributed or transmitted in any form or by any means, or stored in a database or retrieval system without the prior written permission of the publisher.

Editor: Jennifer Jones, Book Ends Editing
Cover: Mariah Sinclair, The Cover Vault

This is a work of fiction. Names, characters, organizations, places, events, and incidents are either products of the author's imagination or are used fictitiously. Any resemblance to actual persons, living or dead, or actual events is purely coincidental.

No part of this work may be reproduced, or stored in a retrieval system, or transmitted in any form or by any means, electronic, mechanical, photocopying, recording, or otherwise, without written permission of the publisher.

Moonlight and Magic: Paranormal Cozy Mystery : a novel / by Molly Fitz and Trixie Silvertale — 1st ed.

[1. Paranormal Cozy Mystery — Fiction. 2. Cozy Mystery — Fiction. 3. Amateur Sleuths — Fiction. 4. Female Sleuth — Fiction. 5. Wit and Humor — Fiction.]

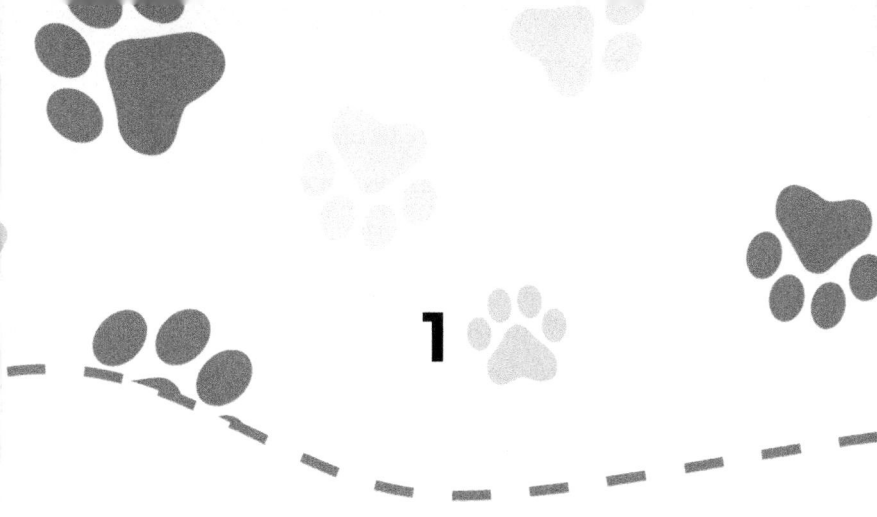

1

Operations were underway for the most buzz-worthy thing to happen at Moonlight Manor since the murder of Beatrix de Haviland. The Gothic mansion and its three resident ghosts, including the self-appointed feline Lord of the Manor, Sir Bogart, were finally going to capitalize on history.

Trust me when I tell you, they took blessed little convincing, and now I couldn't be more thrilled to serve as mistress to the haunted manor. Banging echoed out front, and I wasn't sure if it was repairs or ghosts. My grand opening was shaping up to be quite the event.

My escape from New York City to the sleepy town in Maine called Misty Meadows had been bumpy at best. But my luck was about to change. There could be no better use for a massive nineteenth-century mansion, rumored to be haunted, than a series of ghostly tours during the spookiest season of the year. All Hallows Eve would never be the same.

Sure, the guests would assume that everything had been done with the proverbial 'smoke and mirrors,' but my trio of ghosts and I would know the truth. The haunting of Moonlight Manor was as real as could be.

It was incredibly fortunate that freckle-faced baker Frannie Clark and I had hit it off before I'd even officially moved to town. She, too, had migrated from the Midwest to the East Coast and done a soul-sucking stint in New York City. Frannie understood me. And more importantly, she didn't force me to give her details I preferred to keep private. She accepted me and supported me, especially when it came to the phantom friends in residence at Moonlight Manor.

Plus, one thing Frannie was absolutely unstoppable at was gathering the troops. She knew everyone in town, knew what they were good at, and knew how to get ahold of them. She'd found someone to help me clean the manor when I moved in, she'd found someone to lend me a car, and best of all, she'd convinced Davis Martin, the ox-shouldered son of the local hardware store owner, to serve as my handyman in exchange for free pastries from her bakery. I tried to offer him money on more than one occasion, but his crooked-grin answer was always the same.

"Keep your money," he said. "Frannie's got me covered."

Yet I'd seen the man eat. How Frannie made enough for him, I didn't understand. I couldn't imagine how she planned to keep Heaven Can Bake afloat with this guy running a tab, but I was extremely grateful for the help, and it was my handyman whose help I needed right now.

"Davis?" I called.

"Out front."

When I caught sight of him, I had to stop on the broad stone terrace in front of the manor and lean against the wrought-iron railing to catch my breath. One would think that the fall weather in Maine would require more clothing than carpenter pants and a skin tight T-shirt drenched with sweat. As I stared at the thirst-trap of a man in my yard, I could barely force myself to swallow. Having this guy around meant I required repeated reminders—I'd sworn off men. After the selfish ex I left behind in

New York, I didn't need the mess in my newly restarted life.

I sighed and tipped my head as I watched Davis wrap an extension cord around his arm. What would it be like to be that lucky, little extension cord?

Davis dropped the coiled cord in his hand and shaded his eyes against the bright sun. "Whaddya need, Syd?"

Blinking, I brought my brain back to the reason I needed to hunt him down. "Um . . . Updates."

He nodded once and picked up a collection of shims. "One sec."

It made me happy to know that things between us had become more casual. At least some of the time. When we first met, he tried to call me Miss Coleman every time, and when I insisted on Sydney, he simply switched to Miss Sydney. However, the old manor home was feeling a lot like owning a boat, which meant there was always something to fix. So Davis and I had fallen into a comfortable rhythm.

He placed the smaller pieces of wood in a neat pile to the side, dropped a handful of wire ends into a bin, and then straightened. "Which updates did you want?"

I stepped toward him, barely able to contain my excitement. "How's it going with the lights? I can absolutely picture what you're saying about the up-lighting making the towers look spooky and mysterious, but I can't wait to see it."

He grinned, and his green eyes held a hint of pride. "Yeah, it'll be great. Did you ever tell spooky stories around the campfire when you were a kid?"

I nodded, but I didn't understand where he was going with his question. Perhaps I was too distracted by his nearness. Yes, that was definitely it.

"Did you ever hold a flashlight under your chin? Changes your whole face. You're gonna freak out when you see what the manor looks like by the end." He picked up the heavy loops of electrical cable and got back to work on the repairs under the porch eaves.

Walking down the granite steps to the circle encompassing the fountain in the front yard, I turned and gazed up at my mansion.

My mansion. Yes, I was getting used to saying it, but I still didn't completely believe it. How had I wound up with a mansion? With towers. *With towers!* I mentally squealed. One day I was grinding it out at a thankless ad agency job, with a secretly sleazy ex, and the next I was living in a haunted mansion.

Life sure had a strange way of guiding us into new adventures. A failure in New York had brought me to

Misty Meadows. It still boggled my mind now and then.

A strange tingle spread across my scalp, interrupting my wool-gathering, and I felt compelled to turn back toward the fountain. I laid my hand on the low wall circling the unused water feature.

"Hey, do you know if this thing runs?" I called over my shoulder before turning around.

Davis scraped the sandy-brown hair back from his sweaty forehead and grinned as he jogged down the steps to join me. "Only one way to find out."

I stepped back and gave him room to work.

He popped open a flat stone access panel and peered inside.

"See anything?"

"No immediate snakes or spiders."

I shuddered. "I should hope not. It's getting a little cold out this season for snakes."

He gave me a squinty-eyed wink and got right to it. There were wrenches, screwdrivers, and at one point even a crowbar, but eventually a trickle of water dripped from the vase that was held by a lady.

I peered up at the statue as the water dribbled over it. "It's sort of working. There's a little water coming out of her pot."

Davis straightened and gazed at me in mock

horror. "Did you just call the eternal vessel of love, held in the arms of the incredibly beautiful goddess Aphrodite, a pot?"

My eyes widened, and I shook my head. "No. Of course not."

His warm laughter softened the blow of my lack of knowledge. "Don't worry. I didn't know either. I overheard Augusta Adams tearing into somebody at the hardware store. Don't ask me how they landed on the topic of an old fountain at Moonlight Manor, but they said something about Diana and a water pitcher, and old Augusta let 'em have it." Then he disappeared into the inner-working of the water feature once more.

I chuckled, but not as easily as Davis. Augusta was something else.

Finally, he gave a triumphant snort. "Ah ha, here it is, you only thought you could hide your inner workings from me . . ." Davis muttered. Then his voice trailed away as my thoughts turned to the others I'd met during my adventure in business-owning.

I'd been warned more than once about Augusta's temper. That woman had an unmatched reputation in town for architectural and historical expertise, and she did not suffer fools on either topic. Plus, she was the founder and sole owner of the Adams School of Colonial Arts. Her fine work had repaired a damaged pane of antique stained glass at the mansion, after someone hurled a rock through. In addition to the repair, she paid the hooligan, Gladys Williams, a personal visit after the incident. Yikes.

If only that had been the last time I'd had a run in with busybody and amateur vandal Gladys Williams. However, since the start of publicizing the haunted mansion tours, I could count on near daily visits from my angry neighbor. How she had so much time on her hands with her own manor, I didn't understand. She had to have staff taking care of things, if she could afford to always be causing problems in my business ventures.

Though, she never had a direct complaint. It was always more of a random threat about a vague violation. If she could be believed, she had the entire book of city codes memorized, and *my* manor was breaking most of them.

It got so bad this past week, I had to call Sheriff Haley Allen out and have the woman officially escorted off my property. Sheriff Allen had been as grim-faced about the ordeal as I'd ever seen her.

Which, in case you're not familiar, meant that the sheriff told the violator that they were never to set foot on the property again, and if they did, they would be arrested and officially charged with trespassing. The way the sheriff explained it to me, was that it was similar to a restraining order, but without getting the courts involved.

Gladys seemed harmless enough, so it sounded like the type of deterrent that would be effective. I hoped the warning worked in a long-term way. Gladys didn't need to have anything to do with my grand opening.

Correction: She didn't need to have any opportunity to foul up my grand opening.

At my feet, Davis grunted. "Off. Found a spider."

"Are you okay?"

"Fine. Fine. Ah, there's the problem." He didn't add anything else.

Another splatter came out of the pot, and I turned to watch the liquid slip down the statue. Davis kept banging.

Additional clanging, screeching, and a strange gurgling thump were followed by a massive spout of water—which caught me square in the face.

Screaming, I jumped back. I scrubbed at my face, already trying to calculate how old the liquid was. How long had it been there inside the fountain? Did it matter?

Davis scrambled out from whatever secret interior fountain panel he'd been working on and covered his mouth. Not necessarily in surprise. It was more to hide his laughter.

"Davis. I'm soaked." I immediately started to shiver in the cool air of autumn.

He jogged to my side of the fountain, scooped an arm around me, and hurried me indoors, into the foyer. "You're freezing. Let's get you into some dry clothes, Miss Coleman."

Through chattering teeth, I admonished him. "For the—the—umpteenth time, Davis, c-c-call me Sydney. You know how much I hate Miss Coleman. And the water is not your fault. I was the one st-st-anding right in front of Aphrodite's b-b-bottomless jug of love or whatever you called it." My whole body quaked with cold. "How long do you think that water was in there? Do you think I need a dose of antibiotics or something?"

He laughed and shook his head. "Oh, no, no antibiotics necessary, Sydney. Water was from further inside the statue than all that. Now you get upstairs and dry off. We can't have you catch your death of a cold right before your grand opening."

I wrapped my arms around myself and vigorously rubbed the goosebumps on my arms. "Th-th-thanks.

Let me know when you get the fountain under control."

He bounded out the front door, still chuckling, and called over his shoulder, "Will do."

Sir Bogart, my feline overlord, appeared next to me on the steps. His silky black fur glowed to perfection and his intelligent yellow eyes sparked with secrets. "I feel quite certain that young man is sweet on you, mistress."

My grimace didn't seem to deter Sir Bogart. So I added, "Not today, Sir Matchmaker. As you know, I have bigger fish to fry."

He shrugged his lithe shoulders and vanished, mumbling something about fish.

I hurried to my bedroom, the blue room, on the second floor, slipped into dry clothes, and twisted my wet hair out of the way. At least the fountain mishap was mechanical and not paranormal. Davis could finish fixing that up with no problem. But if I was going to make any progress on my final checklist, I needed to get up to the attic and mine for more treasures. I'd set a $150 budget for decorations, and if I had any chance of sticking to the budget, the rest of the dusty décor would have to be found on-site and repurposed.

I scanned my second-floor room, checking for

something large enough to carry items back down out of the attic above the third floor. My laundry hamper looked about the right size to carry a load of fantastic finds. I dumped my dirty clothes onto the floor—to be honest, most of them were already there, paused en route to the washing—and headed toward the third level and the only other robin's-egg-blue glass handle that had called to me on my first visit to the manor.

The little door to the attic had the same gorgeous blue glass knob my bedroom had. Cobalt glass must be the way to my heart, and I imagined where else I could tuck cobalt accents on the second and third floors. Someday.

Yet a mere foot from the narrow door leading to my attic, a disconcerting interruption derailed my decorating plans. I frowned at the angry sounds coming from outside the manor.

Now what? At this rate, I'd never complete the finishing touches on the manor.

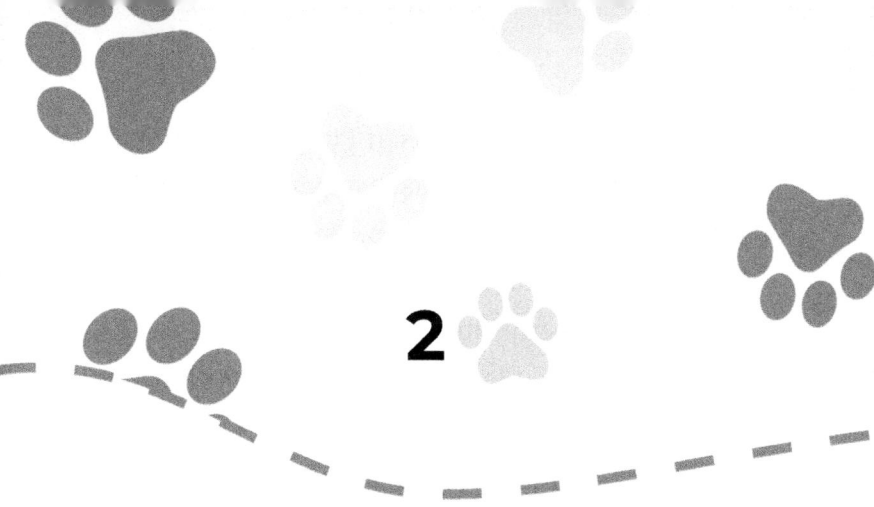

2

Raised voices in the backyard grew louder, and I cringed as I recognized the robust voice. Historical expert and restoration goddess Augusta Adams was lighting into someone. And it didn't sound like mercy was on her mind.

I placed the hamper beside the entry to the attic. Hurrying down the multi-level stairs and to the rear of the manor, I burst through the door-less back entry and stepped right into a heated argument between Augusta and my horrible, sometimes violent neighbor, Gladys Williams.

It hadn't yet come to blows, so I stopped short to watch before baling off into the middle of the altercation.

Augusta swung her arm wildly between them.

"Get off this property, Gladys. If I told you once, I told you a thousand times. What happens at Moonlight Manor is none of your concern. None of it. The feud that started a century and a half ago, is over. They locked the property lines down seventy years ago. The maps are on file with the county if you don't believe me."

Gladys glared daggers at Augusta.

Augusta's face was bright red as she fumed, holding a hammer in her non-gesturing arm. "Well?"

Gladys snorted and then angrily waved a walking stick directly in that fuchsia face. "You wouldn't know a property line from a clothesline. And you might have the rest of the town fooled with your cheap imitations, but I know what you're up to, Adams. You're as sneaky as your dead uncle ever was."

At the mention of her deceased relative, Augusta raised the hammer in her left hand and rather than shouting, her voice went deadly quiet. "Gladys, I'm going to give you exactly thirty seconds to haul your troublemaking rear end back over to your broken-down excuse for a house. And after that, I can't be held responsible for my actions."

The defiant Gladys Williams seemed to shrink in

size. She lowered her cane and hightailed it into the underbrush.

I caught my bottom lip between my teeth to keep from yelling out to Gladys to stay off my property. Gladys had surely gotten the point, and Augusta didn't need any egging on.

At that moment, Davis came around the corner, looked once at the retreating woman, met my eyes, and winked. Without a word, he trotted back around to the front side of the property as though the fight between the two older women was the most normal thing in the entire world—or maybe he simply didn't want to cross either of them.

The fire raging in Augusta's sharp eyes faded as Gladys's signature mustard-colored coat vanished beyond the underbrush. Her gaze fell on me, and the blush of anger was replaced with a quick flash of shame. "I'm sorry you had to see that, Sydney."

I took a deep breath in and let it out slowly. "It's all right. She's been over several times since she found one of the flyers for the haunted mansion tours. I don't know what she has against me, but she's bound and determined that I don't make enough money to stay here." Plastering a wan smile on my face, I said, "Never a dull moment around Moonlight Manor."

Augusta dropped her hammer on a stack of nearby planks that were ready to be installed in the refurbished gazebo and walked toward me with a kind smile. "Try not to take it personally. The Williams family is one of the oldest in the county. Almost as old as the family who built your manor—the Blodfyss clan. Why the two of them insisted on settling side-by-side, when they had nothing but absolute hatred for one another, history has failed to tell us. Even the family stories don't tell us much. However, the bitter land disputes have existed as far back as I know. The Williamses even set fire to the Blodfyss chicken coop at the peak of the dispute. Legend has it the Blodfyss sisters called rain down from the sky to put out the flames."

I stepped forward eagerly, ready to take in more history for our haunted tours. "So they were real witches?"

Augusta laughed. "Not a chance. I'm sure they had a bucket brigade or something similar, but that's not a very interesting story. If you were the Williams, and you were intent on disparaging your neighbors and seeing them run off their land, rumors about witches would be far more effective." Her hard expression made it clear she did not condone such lies or actions.

Shrugging my shoulders, I also nodded in agreement. "Makes sense." I walked toward the gazebo and smiled appreciatively, laying my hand on a smooth place in the supporting timbers. "This looks great. Will it be finished in time for the grand opening?"

Augusta tipped her head as though considering how much work had been done and how much remained. "Not quite. We're about a week behind schedule. But Frannie said you weren't having the big feast until Mischief Night."

"That's right. I was hoping to have a little time to decorate it, but the woodwork is so beautiful I'm having second thoughts." There were no actual second thoughts, but I'd been warned about how defensive Augusta could get and was not interested in drawing her wrath. Especially after what I'd just witnessed.

"Not a problem. We should have you ready to go weekend after this one, and I'll send one of my students out with hay bales and shocks of corn."

"Thank you. That sounds great." I'd pictured spooky ghosts and possibly plastic bats, but I knew Augusta was eager to keep everything, including the décor, historically accurate. That was the downside of working with her. However, the upside was her meticulous craftsmanship and reliable work ethic.

The same could not be said about the contractor I'd hired to repair the back door . . . the now *missing* back door.

Normally, Davis handled all of my repair needs, but he'd referred me to someone else because the entire door jamb had to be replaced, and he wasn't comfortable assessing possible structural damage. I couldn't have cared less, as long as there was a door in place, but he assured me if it wasn't done right, I'd have to repair it again sooner rather than later. My budget was tight to nonexistent. So it made sense to do it once and do it right.

Augusta looked at the unfinished door and walked toward me. Her hand rested on my shoulder. "I need to grab some lunch. Don't worry about Rodney. He's probably sleeping one off, but he should be here in the next hour or so. The man does good work. The only reason I don't use him regularly is the reliability. But I know you're on a budget, honey."

With that, she exited through the side yard, and I stomped back into the house in a darker mood than when I'd bolted out. I called out to the empty hallways, "Does everyone in town know every detail of my miserable life?"

"I believe your friend, Francesca Clark, has kept your secrets regarding Lucas and your unseemly exit from New York." Sir Bogart appeared and fixed me with a haughty stare, and I slumped into a chair in the corner of the kitchen.

"But there is no shame in being on a budget," Sir Bogart added.

"Do not ever call her that. You know as well as I do she prefers Frannie." My shoulders drooped. "But you're right. She's been nothing but trustworthy and honest." And maybe there wasn't anything shameful in being constrained by a budget.

The bass gong of the doorbell echoed throughout the manor, and I hoped it was Rodney arriving to fix the blasted rear exit before I welcomed wild critters as my first haunted tour guests. A random raccoon would certainly send me screaming.

"Rodney, I hope that's you," I muttered under my breath.

It wasn't, but the surprise was more welcome.

"Frannie. We were just talking about you." I opened one of the large double doors and motioned for her to come in.

She carried a lovely pink pastry box, and that was always a welcome sight to combat the downturn in my mood. "Oh, who's we?"

"Augusta." I jerked a hand over my shoulder. "She's been working on the gazebo in the back." I wasn't about to tell her about the conversation with Sir Bogart. She tolerated my ghostly sidekicks, but they still sort of made her uncomfortable.

She grinned as she slipped by me, with the pink box in her hands, and made her way to the kitchen. "Can't wait to see what Augusta cooks up for that dreamy gazebo."

I trailed after her. Since I loosened my New York City stranglehold on my diet, and started walking every day, I'd been able to enjoy some of the wonderful treats I'd denied myself for the last seven years. And, so far, I was still fitting into my pants. I was happier than I'd been in decades.

Frannie sat down at the sturdy oak table in the corner of the kitchen, and I started a fresh pot of coffee brewing.

I nodded to the box. "What did you bring me? Please tell me it's caramel-apple cupcakes."

She laughed as she opened the box. "Sorry to disappoint, but I brought you some tastings so we could make the final decisions about the menu for the Halloween feast. I don't have much time. I've got a gal from the high school covering for me, but she has to get back for her fifth period."

I grabbed the chair across from Frannie, and she carefully extracted each item from the large box. "I was hoping to hit on a certain theme. But I sort of went all over the place. You pick your favorites, and I'll make it work."

My mouth watered, and I couldn't wait to sample her wares.

She placed each treat in a row in front of me as she announced it. "Here are the sweet treats: spellbook s'more cookies; vampire chocolate chip cookie sandwiches; eyeball bark; and pumpkin patch brownies."

A snicker escaped me. "What great names. Everything looks so delicious. How do you expect me to choose?"

Frannie grinned. "Hold on, there's more. For savory items, I made individual *dragon* meat hand pies and put a little green food coloring in the dough."

She pushed one toward me, and it looked adorable. "I've also made individual barbecue ranch chicken shepherd's pie with spooky ghost toppers."

The little mashed potato ghost, with peas for eyes, smiled up at me, and I clasped my hands in front of my chest. "Frannie, they're amazing," I said with an appreciative sigh. What incredible creativity.

She continued to pull items from the box. "This one has cheese, but I can make it without."

Jumping up, I headed for the cupboard. "Let me get a couple of plates, a knife, and forks. If I'm going to try everything, I'm going to have to take smaller portions." While I was up, I poured the coffee and grabbed us each a place setting.

She made a flourish as she pulled another from the box and placed it on the table. "Last but not least, these ghost strawberries are easy to make, and kids love them."

I grabbed one and took a large bite. "Kids *and* grown-ups. Those are definitely on the list. Love them."

She chuckled and made a note on her phone. She pretty much beamed the entire time I sang the praises of her skills in the bakery.

We powered through the rest of the tasty treats and had most of the menu decided by the time Frannie had to leave.

Walking her to the front door, pumpkin patch brownie in hand, I patted my stomach. "I won't have to eat for the rest of the week. Thank you for coming up with such wonderful stuff."

She waved, jumped in her pink Suzuki Samurai—a perfect match to the pink bakery boxes she used for her goodies, and zipped back into town.

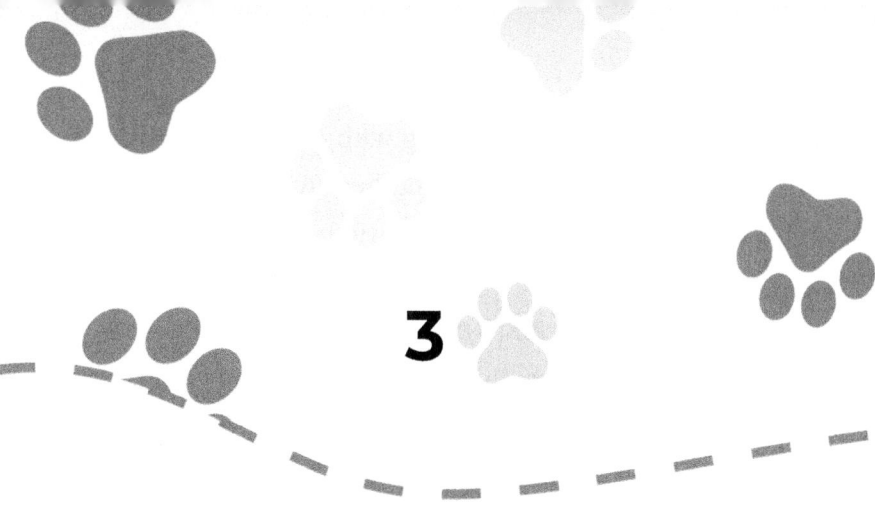

3

Finally, there was hammering at the back door. I felt certain Augusta hadn't returned from her lunch yet, so perhaps the elusive Rodney had arrived at last. A part of me wondered why Davis had recommended Rodney for the job. But if Misty Meadows was anything, it was filled with kind people. Maybe Davis was trying to share work with the down-on-his-luck ex-contractor. It certainly sounded like the way Davis liked to do things.

I made my way to the rear of the house. Yet before I'd even reached the mudroom to check where the noise originated, another argument broke out.

When I marched through the unfinished opening at the rear of my home, I was unsurprised to see Gladys Williams shaking her walking stick at my contractor. What was wrong with her? The intrusive woman simply couldn't mind her own business. And yet I was more than a little curious to hear what she had to say

"You're a liar and a cheat," she snarled at the man Davis had recommended. "I've never been so happy to see anyone go out of business in my life. I don't know how you got another contractor's license, but you can bet your britches I will see you fail again before I let you make another dirty dime off the innocent residents of Misty Meadows."

Interesting. Maybe there was something to the saying that the enemy of my enemy is my friend. If I didn't know better, it almost sounded like Gladys Williams was looking out for my best interests. Could it be so?

Rodney dropped his hammer through the loop on this tool belt, widened his stance, and crossed his arms defiantly. "Listen, you old hag, you ruined my life. I lost everything because of you. My business, my job, my family. All of it. So don't you worry about all that, I couldn't get another contractor's license if I tried. This is handyman work. You don't need a license for that. Not around here. So you take your interfering behind back to your own land before I call Sheriff Allen. Everyone knows you've been escorted off this property for trespassing ever since you broke that window. You're no saint yourself, and you aren't allowed here. Ol' snake in the grass Gladys."

She raised her stick, and it appeared she was about to have another go at Rodney. I didn't think she'd be brave—or bonkers—enough to actually hit a grown man, so I didn't put myself between them. Still, even though I didn't like the sound of an unlicensed contractor doing my repairs, he had come recommended by someone I trusted and I needed him to finish the job.

But my house needed to have a rear door in place, and I was running out of time before the grand opening. So I stepped forward and positioned myself between the warring parties. "Look, Mrs. Williams. You and I have no quarrel. The original owners and your ancestors may not have been able to agree on anything, but that's no reason for you to come onto my property and harass my workers. Rodney is doing the job he was hired to do. And I expect you to let him do it."

She narrowed her gaze and shook her walking stick at me. "No two-bit witch is going to tell me what to do."

My mouth hung slack for a moment, but then I located my inner New York City girl. I stepped menacingly toward the intruder and arched an eyebrow at her. "Tell you what, Gladys. Why don't I give Sheriff Allen a call? I think she'd be very interested to find out that you're violating her no trespass order for the second time today. Maybe she'll even find you a spot in one of her cells." I paused. "And just to be clear, if I ever find you on my property again, you'll regret it."

She blinked as though surprised I'd stood up to her stick-shaking, and for a long moment, I thought she might go off again.

But I kept my tongue, and I didn't bother to argue with her claim that I was a witch. What difference did it make if she thought that? Being rumored a witch might help those interested in my tours. Let her think whatever she liked as long as it kept her out of my hair and away from my haunted mansion preparations.

Finally, she relented and skulked off to the distant row of pine trees once more. If I never saw that woman again, it would be too soon.

A soft voice spoke behind me. "Thanks, Miss Coleman. Not a lot of folks around here defend me anymore. I appreciate it."

Not wanting to give the wrong impression, I felt compelled to clarify my actions. "Look, Rodney. I never listen to rumors or gossip. Instead, I wait for people to prove themselves to me. And I got rid of Gladys because I need you to finish the door, and she was in the way of that. I hope there won't be any more interruptions or late starts, and I sincerely hope you make good use of what time we have left today. I have a grand opening riding on it."

He swallowed hard and nodded. "Yes, miss. I'll do my best."

I pressed my lips together and nodded. The last thing I needed was anyone—especially not a contractor who worked for me—thinking I was a softy. No, negligence would not be tolerated.

As I stepped into the kitchen to clean up the mess Frannie and I had left, the ghostly cook was already hard at work. She finished scrubbing one of the used coffee cups and floated across the room to the cabinet it belonged in.

I rushed forward and took the coffee mug from her. "I can do that, Velma. Aren't you supposed to be helping Norman with the cobwebs?"

Velma clasped her hands behind her back and bobbed her head in my direction as she hovered over the grounds. "Yes, miss. Norman says he can't do it, miss. He won't."

Norman and I had already had this discussion

once, but it appeared that he would need further encouragement. Scrunching my nose, I put my hands on my hips. "Where is he?"

"Foyer."

"Very well." When I walked into the foyer, I discovered Norman, spirit of the manor's last butler, collecting the bags of faux spider web and putting them in a trash bin. "Excuse me, Norman."

He dropped the can with a clatter and floated several feet off the ground. "Yes, madam. How may I assist?"

I put my hands on my hips as I faced the ghost butler. "Well, I thought it was fairly clear how you could assist me. I specifically asked you and Velma to hang spider webs all over the grand staircase, and from the chandeliers and sconces—in the entry and the ballroom. There will be plenty of opportunity to clean up next month, after the tours." My mouth tightened around the last word.

He drifted toward me and wrung his hands repeatedly. "I swore to serve you, madam. But it goes against every fiber of my being to create disorder."

"Hey, I understand. But try to remember there are no fibers to your being. You're a ghost. Yes, you are still serving as butler of the manor, but wouldn't you agree that the rules have changed?"

He nodded, but he continued to wring his transparent hands. "I know you're right, madam, but it is most difficult. I have behaved a particular way for a long time. Perhaps a distraction would help me overcome the obstacle in my mind."

"What type of distraction?"

"May I straighten your room, madam?"

I gaped at the butler. That had to be the nicest way anyone had ever told me I was a slob. I had forced myself to be organized for so many years to please Lucas. When I officially moved into Moonlight Manor, I let my hair—and everything else—down. "You know what, Norman. That actually sounds wonderful. The bedding needs to be washed. I'm sure there's clothing that could use a scrub, and—"

"I have a rather particular process, madam. With your permission, I shall begin at once."

"You have my permission, Norman. And my thanks."

He gave a perfunctory bow and vanished.

When I returned to the kitchen, Velma was drying the last plate. "Any luck, miss?"

"Not exactly. Why don't I help you with the cobwebs, and we'll leave Norman to do what he does best."

Velma glanced mischievously at me. "Straighten

the ever-loving life out of everything?" She placed a hand over her mouth and giggled.

"Precisely." I made a face. "At least he's good at it."

She lowered her hand. "Indeed, miss."

We dumped the packages of faux webbing from the wastepaper bin and began the laborious process of stretching and hanging. Although, I had to admit that hanging the webbing with the help of a ghost was far easier than endless trips up and down a ladder.

Hours passed, and we made fabulous progress and only had to endure the insults of Sir Bogart twice. He shared Norman's views on the décor and made no secret of it. Nevertheless, we worked long into the night, determined not to fail when we were so close to a grand triumph.

4

Most people found the creaking attic of a one-hundred-fifty-year-old mansion spooky—or at the very least unwelcoming. However, since I arrived at Moonlight Manor, I'd always felt most myself in the dimly lit peaks of my estate. It was a treasure trove of history and interesting items.

For most of the next morning, fueled by strong coffee and stubbornness, I took to hunting through the vast array of antiques, hoping to find more trinkets to use as set dressing for my haunted house attraction. Velma and I had dedicated much of the night before, decorating and "spookifying" as much as we could, but I'd woken early and gotten started as quickly as possible. We had no time to waste.

There was a long list of last-minute preparations, and I was determined to get through it before the first tour group arrived. I had a silver chalice with a set of ornate silver spoons. Though, the search of the attic had also unearthed a particularly interesting book, but I needed more information about it before I could be sure it was okay to place out on display. All these items would work nicely with the other items we already had.

"Sir Bogart? Velma? Norman?" I called to the empty space. "I have some questions."

Despite having lived with the ghosts for several weeks, the sudden appearance of a glowing, majestic black feline always made my heart stutter. When we first met, he insisted on using his full title: His Royal Felineness, Bogart the First, the Only, the Eternal.

Since I'd helped him solve a murder, we'd grown closer, and he allowed me to refer to him more informally. "Hey, Bogey. What do you think of the decorating downstairs?"

His velvet rope tail flicked, and he sauntered to the window and leapt up onto the sill. "I believe you and Cook have done a marvelous job of preparing the estate. I may not comprehend why mortals wish to pay good money to be frightened amidst dust and cobwebs, but if it will assist you with your mortal needs, mistress, then I approve."

His approval surprised me, but before I had the opportunity to offer my thanks, Velma and Norman appeared on either side of the shimmering black cat.

I nodded to the trio and then raised the old volume I'd found. "Thanks for popping in. I found this interesting old book up here, and I was wondering if it would make a good prop on that large table in the entryway? It looks like some kind of recipe book. Do any of you know anything about it?"

At the mention of recipes, Velma drifted forward, leafed through the tome, and stared at the aged pages within the leather-bound book. "Them don't look like no recipes I ever seen, miss."

I closed the book, pointed to the symbols carved into the thick leather cover, and held it out for the others to see. "What do you think these mean? A star in a circle and these squiggly lines."

Sir Bogart leapt from the windowsill and slinked across the floor, tilting his head as he drew closer. "That is no star, mistress. It is a pentacle, and the markings to which you referred as squiggly lines are the symbols of the zodiac. It would appear you have discovered the Blodfyss Grimoire."

"What?" Something in the tone of his voice made

me drop the book onto the lid of the trunk and back away. "What is a grimoire?"

"A book of spells, if you will."

I frowned at the book, still resting on the lid of the trunk.

Sir Bogart continued. "Perhaps you recall my previous mistress, Beatrix Blodfyss de Haviland. She chose de Haviland as a stage name and dropped the dark past associated with the Blodfyss surname. And as I have mentioned, a distant heir thought the Moonlight Manor moniker would sell the property more quickly and renamed it thusly long after my mistress's passing."

My mouth twisted. "Well, I don't know about quickly, Bogey. Sounds like it still took about fifty years to find the right sucker to buy."

Norman stepped to my defense. "I beg you not to refer to yourself in that way, madam. It may have been fate that brought you to us, but if not for you, we'd never have solved the murder of our former mistress. You freed her spirit from its torture—trapped in between the worlds. We consider you a gift."

I smiled and blushed. "Thank you, Norman. I'm grateful we all met, but I'm still feeling nervous about this haunted house venture. If it ends as badly as the bed-and-breakfast disaster, I'm worried I may not be able to keep the place. My bank balances are dwindling, and we can't make it through another quarter without some kind of income." I winked at the trio. "After all, I'm not a useful specter haunting this place."

Norman clasped his hands behind his back and offered me a slight bow. "I think the manor looks spectacular, madam. It will be the perfect combination of elegance and fright. The tours will be a success, I'm certain of it."

"I hope you're right. So what do you think?" I looked over the trio of faces and gestured to the volume in question. "Should I use this book as part of the decorations?"

Sir Bogart jumped onto the trunk and circled the book suspiciously. "There are many stories of the original Blodfyss sisters, and, I must say, I cannot recall a single happy ending. I fear this grimoire could be the source of tragedy rather than entertainment."

My scowl had no impact on the feline specter. "You can't be serious, Bogey. Are you saying *this* book actually has magical powers?"

The tip of his tail crooked. "Not the book, per se.

But the spells within its pages could be potent, even dangerous, in the wrong hands."

Acting braver than I felt, I laughed, swiped the book from the trunk lid, and paged through it. "Nonsense. It's just rumors and stories meant to scare children. There's no such thing as witches or magic."

The majestic cat dropped back onto his haunches and fixed me with his glowing eyes. "Mistress, can you honestly speak to a ghost out of one side of your mouth and deny the existence of magic with the other?"

To my credit, I didn't bat an eye even when my insides knotted as I processed his words. "You have a point, Bogey. But I'm definitely not a witch. So, I don't think we have anything to worry about. The verses inside mean nothing to me. So I'll put the book on the table, and everyone will think it's a prop. No one will be the wiser, and everything will be fine."

His whiskers wiggled nervously, and his tail snapped back and forth. "I would advise against it, mistress."

"Well, what do Velma and Norman think of my plan?" When I glanced at them, their expressions were tight and they studied the floor between us. I didn't have to guess at their feelings on the matter.

Sir Bogart blinked but had the decency to remain quiet.

When I shifted my hands, the grimoire fell open in one of my palms. I drew my fingers over the yellowed page, fascinated by the spots and stains on the parchment. What kind of stories could the grimoire tell? The drafty attic creaked, and time seemed to stop as I stared.

"Miss?" Velma sounded hesitant, as though she thought she might be interrupting. "Are you all right, miss?"

"Oh, I'm fine." I tapped my fingers on a rather strange passage in the lower portion of one of the pages. "Here, I'll read this wild poem to you, and you tell me if this sounds like anything even close to the realm of possibility." I tilted the book toward the light filtering through the round windows in the dormers.

> *"When the waxing harvest moon rises high,*
> *And clouds vanish from the autumn night sky,*
> *The walls of sweet Blodfyss will live and breathe.*
> *Ages of justice from the heart will seethe.*
> *All who dare to enter with ill intent,*
> *Will relive their crime and death's punishment."*

The wind howled around the corners of the manor, and the shimmering apparition of the feline vanished as a disembodied voice called from the ether. "You were warned, mistress."

The overly cautious cat made me chuckle. I snapped the volume closed, grabbed a couple of other interesting artifacts, and crept down the steep staircase to the third level.

"Do you need anything else from us, miss?" Velma asked, and Norman floated a little closer to hear my answer.

"No, you can go back to whatever you were doing. Thank you, both."

After they popped out of view, I loaded the hamper to take my finds downstairs.

I placed the tarnished silver chalice on a side table we'd set on the first landing of the imperial staircase, along with some antique silver spoons and newly purchased plastic bones. Carrying the tome down to the ground level, across the polished parquet flooring, I approached the round walnut table under the massive chandelier in the grand foyer.

Before I could place the new item, I had to move a few other things to make room for the grimoire, including a plastic squirrel skeleton with a nut clutched in its front paws. Each addition added so much to the décor.

Stepping back to admire my display, I called out in a sing-song voice, "It's perfect."

I hurried to the kitchen to fetch a dish towel to roll up and place under the old book, so it would be propped up at an angle and be more visible during the tours. It really was the centerpiece of everything on the table.

My eyes trailed across the grand entrance, the massive chandelier, and the freedom I'd purchased for myself with this unexpected relocation. The heartache of getting dumped by my ex had turned into an impressive exodus to the countryside.

The painful memories of my abrupt exit from New York were fading, and I found more and more little ways to make Misty Meadows my new home. Having the company of the ghosts was oddly comforting. They kept me from what might turn into an oppressive loneliness, so far into the countryside without anyone else living in the old mansion.

A deep chiming of the doorbell fortunately interrupted any more unnecessary trips down memory lane. As I approached the grand double doors of the front entrance, I glanced at the newly repaired stained-glass panel and smiled. Augusta Adams really was an expert artisan. I didn't think there was a soul on earth, with the possible exception of her, who could tell the difference between the wholly original panel on the left and the repaired panel on the right. She'd found an exact match to a troublesome milky-blue colored glass as well, and the delicate oak leaves were flawless.

Reaching for the large brass handle, I smiled as I opened the door. "Frannie. I could smell those caramel-apple cupcakes a mile away. Come in. Come in. What brings you out to the manor so soon? I mean, you were just here with samples," I teased.

She smiled and glanced around at all the decorations festooning my home. "All the decorations weren't up last time." She paused. "It's really shaping up in here, Sydney." She adjusted the messy bun that held back her bright-red curls and grinned. "It actually looks beautiful and not too terrifying."

I nudged her gently with my elbow as she carried another pink pastry box of cupcakes to the kitchen. "Well, you don't have to spend a lot of money on decorations when you have an attic full of ancient artifacts and a house full of real ghosts."

We chuckled together.

She placed the pink box on the table and grinned. "I saw the vehicle when I pulled up. Is it new? I don't remember seeing it yesterday. It looks like the same thing as what you borrowed from Craig."

"It sure is. When I sold off those bottles of rare wine from the hidden cellar under the ballroom, I had enough to buy a cheap used vehicle, and I told Craig how much I liked driving his."

Frannie's eyes widened. "So that's—"

"Yup. Craig sold me his SUV. He said he'd had a good year on the lobster boat, and he wanted a reliable four-wheel-drive truck before winter. So I'm the proud owner of Blue Bell."

She chuckled. "It's cute how he says *lobstah*, don't you think? Don't you like how he says *lobstah*?"

I shrugged and smiled. "Frannie, I told you, I've sworn off men—at least for now."

She winked. "Whatever you say, but word around town is that Davis Martin has been making a lot of trips to Moonlight Manor. I saw him yesterday, and he was here again today, working on the fountain when I pulled up."

At the mention of my behemoth handyman, my

cheeks blushed. "Again, Davis is a wonderful handyman, and he's been a huge help getting this place ready, and I thank you for putting me in contact with him. But there's nothing going on between us, and he even referred me to someone else to replace the broken door into the garden."

"Really? Who?" She pressed brew on the coffeemaker.

"I think his name is Rodney Finley? Something like that. Anyway, he's a local contractor. And since the entire frame needs to be repaired, and a damaged panel replaced on the door, Davis felt more comfortable having a contractor do the work."

A look of concern pinched Frannie's features. "Are you sure it's Rodney Finley? If I'm not mistaken, he was involved in a bit of a hoopla a couple of years back. I thought he lost his contractor's license."

Maybe the rantings of my troublesome neighbor-enemy were closer to the truth than I'd thought. "Well, it's only a door, and the price was right. You know how I have to watch my pennies around here. Davis recommended him, so I'm willing to give him the benefit of the doubt for now."

She nodded. "Yeah, I get it. I sure hope this haunted house attraction takes off. You could have several big weekends of ticket sales before

Halloween. If you play your cards right, that money could tide you over for a couple months."

I nodded and breathed a heavy sigh of relief. "At least I was able to pay off my credit cards with some of the wine money. Plus, since I paid cash for this place, I just need to keep the lights on. You know?"

"I do. I was lucky to have a big nest egg when I started the bakery, but it took a long time to make it profitable. If this haunted mansion thing goes well, maybe you can do something Scrooge-themed for Christmas."

Rubbing my fingers across my lips, my eyes drifted away as I imagined ghostly holiday themes. "Yeah, that's a great idea. Fingers crossed. Our grand opening is tonight."

The distant sound of hammering interrupted our girl's cupcake catch-up. "Hold on, sounds like Rodney's working on the door. I'll be right back." I left Frannie to pour the coffee as I hurried to check in with my workman.

He looked even more sullen today than yesterday, or the first time he'd come out to the property to pick up the broken door and take measurements. Maybe he was having an off day, happened to the best of us. Gladys Williams's stick-shaking could send anybody into a snit. At least he arrived earlier than he'd managed to get himself here previously.

I studied his profile a moment before speaking. "Good morning, Rodney. Can I get you a cup of coffee or anything?"

He jumped at the sound of my voice. "Oh, good morning, Miss Coleman. You scared me."

"Looks like my haunted mansion is already working." He didn't laugh at my attempted joke. So I added, "Please call me Sydney."

He nodded. "Then it's 'good morning, Sydney.' I got most of the prep work done yesterday, so I'll have this door hung in a jiffy and be out of your hair."

"Great. Will you be joining us for the festivities tonight?"

A cloud passed over his face. "Nope. Gotta take my kids shopping for costumes."

"Of course. Well, if they're old enough to enjoy a haunted house, bring them by. No charge."

Rodney glanced toward the edge of my property and shook his head. "Thank you, but I don't think that's a good idea."

"I'm sure you know best. I appreciate you getting the door repaired so quickly. The weather is getting colder, and I definitely want to make sure we can lock this place up tight when we're paying to heat it."

He nodded and resumed his work. A clear sign that this conversation was over.

I returned to the kitchen to finish gossiping with Frannie. "Looks like he'll have that door in this morning, and that's the last repair on my list."

"Then it's on to your grand opening."

I winced. "So much depends on this going well, it's hard not to be nervous."

"A few butterflies are understandable." She lifted her mug and clinked it against mine. "Congratulations on your new venture."

"Thanks." We enjoyed our luscious cinnamon buttercream covered cupcakes in silence, and I relished each and every bite. New York Sydney didn't control everything about me anymore. Moving to Maine had provided some of the best changes in my life.

A happy sigh escaped. "We should start every day like this. Thanks for making the trip out and setting the tone for an amazing grand opening day. Will I see you tonight?"

Frannie nodded with a full mouth and wiped a little buttercream from her freckled face. "Wouldn't miss it."

I walked her to the front door, and she glanced at the antique book on the round table. "That's a great prop. You really have an eye for this sort of thing, Sydney. I can't wait to see what the ghosts have planned for tonight."

Patting her on the back, I accompanied her down the broad granite steps toward her pink pastry box on wheels. "You and me both."

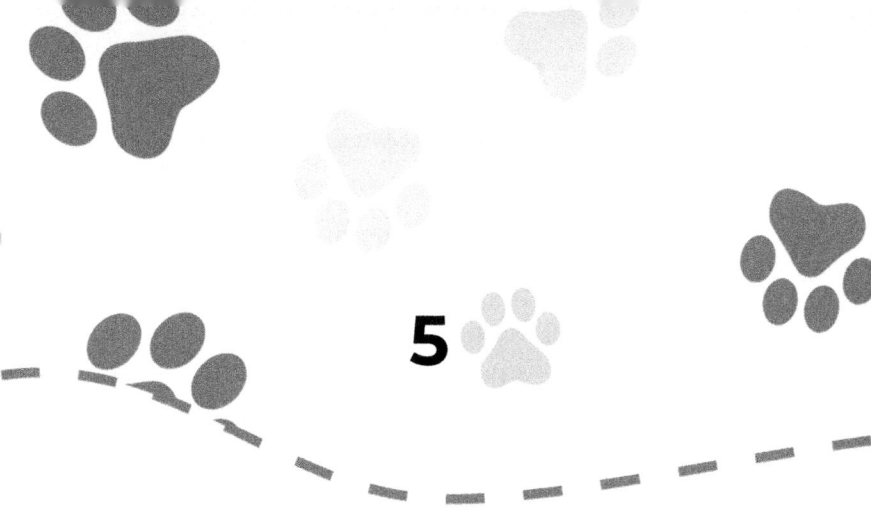

5

The autumn wind cleared the clouds from the darkening sky, and a waxing harvest moon rose brightly over the manor. Smiling with pride, I turned on the lights illuminating the drive, the circle, and the elegant fountain. The goddess Aphrodite poured love out to the world from her massive pitcher and the spray of water glistened in the moonlight. Guests would be arriving any minute. My shoulders were tense with anticipation, but I planned on enjoying the grand opening.

"Bogey?"

In a flash, the regal ghost cat appeared. "Yes, mistress."

"Please remember, we want more guests to come

and enjoy the attraction next weekend. So keep your frights lighthearted."

A sly grin revealed his gleaming fangs—I was not allowed to call them "canines," not without receiving an earful from his Royal Felineness.

"If fright is what they seek, they will not be disappointed." Bogey vanished with a pop.

I shook my head. His words neither comforted nor surprised me. He may refer to me as mistress, but after more than five decades as a ghost, Sir Bogart was the true master of Moonlight Manor, and he did as he pleased.

Each tour group would be led by yours truly. I'd gathered tidbits of interest from the history of Blodfyss Estate, now Moonlight Manor, and would sprinkle them in between the spooky stuff. Since the original inhabitants had been accused of being witches, the All Hallows Eve scares were practically built in. Norman, Velma, and Sir Bogart had several frights planned for the tour. They refused to give me any details on their schemes, so my screams would be as realistic as our guests'.

The tickets were available to purchase online and at Frannie's bakery, Heaven Can Bake, and had sold well with Frannie pushing them. Online sales for our grand opening had been slightly slower but had still been enough to encourage me. Our grand opening night was mostly sold out.

Tours started on the hour, beginning at 8:00 p.m. Four tours each night. Weekends only. I'd promised each group a forty-five minute tour of terror, which allowed me a fifteen-minute break between the groups. We had a lot riding on the success of the experience.

The first tour would start in ten minutes. So I straightened my 1800s garb, courtesy of my mysterious attic, and headed toward the fountain to wait, thankful the coolness of the weather offset the extra historical layers I wore.

As the guests for the first tour arrived, I mentally recited everything I'd learned from Mia, my realtor, about the architecture. Extending my hand, I lifted my chin slightly in my best imitation of a proper mistress of the manor.

"As you can see, Moonlight Manor is clad in rusticated granite and the front elevation is composed of two distinct towers. The one on the right is cylindrical and adds a little bump-out to the first floor drawing room and second floor main suite. The top of that round tower is trimmed with what's called egg-and-dart molding and capped by a conical Tyrollean roof. Technically, that was more of a Scottish Baronial feature, but because the home was built during the Gothic Revival period, it's still classified as Gothic."

The gathering crowd was unimpressed by the commentary, so I added a fresh twist of my own. "It's said that during a full moon, the gargoyles come to life. Perhaps they'll grace you with their presence tonight."

A wave of excited murmurs spread through the group, and anticipation thrummed through the air. At the back of the group, two attendees whispered furiously back and forth, probably guessing at what might happen next.

Now I had them, and I arched an eyebrow to keep my expression from turning into a cheesy grin. Keeping the dramatic mood was of the utmost importance now.

"Welcome to Moonlight Manor," I pronounced, drawing out the syllables.

An expectant hush spread over the attendees. There were fifteen people in my first group, and I would pay careful attention to their comments and reactions. I'd learned a lot about the importance of market research and reading the room during my time as a powerful social media icon at the Aconite Agency back in New York. I intended to make little tweaks to my speech with each tour, based on audience engagement. By the end of this grand opening, I would have everything running like a well-oiled machine. Haunted mansion tours at Moonlight Manor would be the next big thing.

I clasped my hands demurely in front of myself. "We'll start your tour in just a moment. I'd like to mention to everyone that this is an actual home, and some areas will be off-limits to guests. Please stay with the tour group and do not touch any of the items on display. Many of these artifacts have historical significance to the manor and would be irreplaceable."

There was a general nod of agreement from the group. All eyes remained on me.

My skirts rustled against the ground as I took a step. "Several frights await you, but no harm. If at any point you feel too nervous or afraid to continue, please let me know. And I will immediately escort you out of the estate."

More nods.

I smiled brightly. "Now. Is everyone ready to begin?"

Murmurs of agreement passed through the crowd. A young couple had dressed up for the occasion in fairly authentic 1800s wardrobe. Some of the children had donned masks or costumes of their favorite animated characters, and the rest wore everyday clothes.

As I turned to begin the tour, footsteps raced across the gravel. "Sorry, I'm late." Frannie waved surreptitiously and shrugged. "Yeast emergency."

"Perfect timing. We're about to begin." I winked at her playfully before straightening my expression and returning to my somber mistress self.

Opening the massive arched doors, I led the way into the manor. As I launched into my speech about the original owners of the estate, the lights in the grand foyer and on the chandelier flickered.

Titters passed through the group, and Sir Bogart appeared atop the round table in the grand foyer, leapt to the parquet floor, and raced up the imperial staircase.

There were screams, clapping, and whispers of delight.

So far, so good.

My shoes clicked against the floor. "If you'll follow me to the ballroom, please."

I could sense the excitement building, and I hoped the guests wouldn't be disappointed. Surely, Velma, Norman, and Bogey had cooked up an amazing show. The success of this place depended on this weekend, and I had placed a lot of trust in them.

As we rounded the corner and entered the grand ballroom, Velma was playing the piano. She kept herself invisible to the guests, but because I was the official mistress of the manor, I could still see her. The eerie music echoed through the hallways.

One of the guests pulled out her phone to take a video. "Look. The piano is playing itself." She panned across the room and commented about the gorgeous drapes and the plastic bats.

A surly teenager shrugged. "Big deal. I could set that up in like five minutes," he said.

I hadn't planned this part, but I was eager to keep the messaging positive, so I improvised. "You may approach the piano and take a closer look."

The guests, even the sassy teen, hesitantly approached. One said, "It's so cold over here."

I pointed inside the grand piano. "This is no player piano. As you can see within, it's a standard grand piano." I gestured to the interior. "No mechanics."

There were some gulps, and everyone backed away slowly. Velma beamed, and her bonnet-covered head bobbed with glee. I winked at her, and as we turned to leave the ghost of my butler, Norman, drifted across the ballroom with a silver tray of freshly made drinks.

What a fabulous idea. I jumped on board immediately. "Anyone care for a beverage?"

The guests all shook their heads, and the murmurs continued.

"If you'll follow me up the imperial staircase, we'll see what visions await in the lavish bedrooms of Moonlight Manor." It was important to repeat the name. I wanted to make sure these guests got it right when they posted on social media. Every post had to lead thrill-seekers here.

As we headed up the stairs, one of the younger children whispered, "This is where the cat went, Mom."

His mother patted his shoulder and shushed him.

I took them to the lavender room and commented on the amethyst glass handle. Then we moved on to the amber room, with, you guessed it, an amber glass door handle, and finally, we approached the burgundy room.

We gathered outside the door, and I turned slowly toward them. The younger child hid behind his mother's leg. The whole manor was quiet, except for the occasional creak of old boards in an old house.

Pausing for the best dramatic effect, I began the manor's darkest tale. At first, I wasn't sure if I was willing to sensationalize Beatrix de Haviland's murder. But Sir Bogart assured me that she loved nothing more than the spotlight in life, and it would amuse her greatly to think that her death would bring her additional fame.

Clasping my hands, I tried to hide the excited shivers rolling through me. "Ladies, gentlemen, and children, I'm about to take you into the burgundy room. You may not know the history of the manor, but famed costume designer Beatrix de Haviland was murdered in this very room. They say if you're quiet, you can hear her spirit speaking to you."

Footsteps creaked in the walkway behind us, but no one was there. My guests were well and truly frightened now, and I twisted the claret glass knob and opened the burgundy room door.

Silently, we entered the room single file, and they crowded together in the corner, far away from the vanity where I described the general details of Miss de Haviland's demise.

At the end, I raised my arms, hoping my trio of haunters were paying attention. "If you're quiet, perhaps we'll meet the souls who remain in Moonlight Manor."

Someone whimpered, and even the teen's eyes had grown as big as saucers.

The first ghost to arrive on the scene was Sir

Bogart. He appeared in the middle of the burgundy and gold duvet and preened his shoulder with absolute disinterest in his audience.

The young boy shouted, "Look. It's the kitty."

"That's Sir Bogart, the beloved cat of Miss de Haviland." I introduced the feline I'd grown quite fond of since I'd purchased the manor. "He remains, to this day, searching for a way to help his mistress pass on to the afterlife." A part of the truth from when I first met Bogey.

One of the mothers shivered and shook her head. Her mouth twisted with sorrow as she considered the cat on the bed.

Bogart continued to ignore the humans, and as I was about to add additional details and take the troop down the secret passage, Velma floated in.

Still invisible to the ticket holders. She approached the sassy teen and whispered in his ear. "Can you help me?"

The young man nearly jumped out of his skin.

A wave of fear passed through the group, and Velma whispered in one other ear, before they rushed toward me and Sir Bogart vanished from the bed.

The young man's eyebrows had lowered so far down his forehead I almost couldn't see his eyes, and I had to clench my teeth to keep from laughing. He certainly couldn't have managed that. No, Moonlight Manor was the only place where real ghosts would whisper in his ears.

"But where is the rumored third ghostly apparition?" I asked. "Perhaps he was the one who ended Beatrix de Haviland's life?" I'd make my apologies to Norman later, if he took offense to my theatrics. "Is he locked in an endless, bitter haunting until the mystery surroundings Beatrix de Haviland's unexplained death is solved?"

Something like rattling chains sounded in the hallway outside the burgundy room, and their gasps echoed throughout the second floor. Another clatter sent the group surging toward me.

Dramatically, I opened the secret passage and warned in my most mysterious voice. "Your only hope is to sneak down this secret passage and escape the ghost's vengeance."

There was practically a stampede for the narrow door, and the group poured inside as quickly as they could, hampered by single-file.

Frannie paused next to me and shivered. "This is fantastic." She pointed to the secret passage and winked. "Just incredible."

The guests hurried through the corridor, and I took my time following. Davis had helped me hang a single strand of fairy lights along the narrow, twisting stairs. I wanted folks to be frightened, but I didn't want any injuries or lawsuits. Following the last guest into the tunnel, I closed the door behind me, plunging the stairs in shadow. Carefully, we all made our way through the passageway.

When I reached the drawing room, I could hear the heavy breathing of my guests, and I knew my trio of specters and I had done a bang-up job. The forty-five minutes had flown by.

Once we were all in the drawing room, I smiled at my unsettled tour members. "Thank you all for coming. I hope you enjoyed your visit to Moonlight Manor. Please tell your friends and feel free to visit us again next weekend. If you purchase tickets for the 11:00 p.m. tour on All Hallows Eve, there will be a feast at midnight in the newly restored gazebo in the garden."

Even though I was doing my best happy tour guide impersonation, the guests were pushing anxiously toward the exit, and I couldn't tell if the event was a success or not.

I led them all back down the front steps to the fountain, and in the golden-orange moonlight, the water pouring from Aphrodite's jug took on an eerie crimson glimmer.

Several of the guests pointed and cried, "It's blood."

Without lingering, they hurried off to their cars, and I smirked. That's actually a good idea. Although, I would hate to ruin the statuary with food coloring. Maybe a cleverly placed light would do the trick, in case the moon wasn't so helpful with the next tour group.

Frannie patted my back and let out a low whistle. "This will be the talk of the town tomorrow. I think you found your 'thing,' Syd. Good luck with the rest of the tours. I have to open early tomorrow, but I'll call you in the afternoon to catch up."

Waving to her as she jogged to her vehicle, I called out, "Thanks for coming."

She waved in return and jumped into her car.

Tires crunched on gravel, and I gazed up at the gargoyles on the parapets. They all seemed to share my satisfied grin.

Hurrying into the manor, I called out to my cohorts. "Bogey? Norman? Velma? You guys were amazing. That was exactly perfect. I don't know what else you have planned for the next tour, but that was fabulous. We'll be sold out by Monday at this rate."

Sir Bogart strutted down the wide staircase. His glowing eyes never left my face as his hips and shoulders rocked in a mesmerizing rhythm. "I am most pleased that we met your expectations, mistress. However, I'm still concerned about leaving the grimoire on display."

I gestured to the old book and shrugged. "People think it's a prop, Bogey. Even Frannie said that. And she knows about you guys."

Velma nodded, and Norman oddly took my side. "I believe it will be fine, Sir Bogart. It is as madam says. These interlopers are far too eager to assume it is all cheap décor and a trick of the lights. I fear none are true believers." He shook his head sadly, and Velma sighed in agreement.

Bogey lifted an eyebrow but offered no additional argument. "We shall prepare for the next group, mistress."

Headlights shone through the stained glass, casting shadows of oak leaves on the wall. "Right. I'll head out to greet them, and you three get to your places."

They vanished in an instant, and I hurried down the dark, granite steps to greet the next group.

With each tour, my confidence grew. My otherworldly assistants expanded their repertoire, and their creativity impressed me. Between the second and third tours, I decided the only way to do any sort of haunted anything was with three ghost besties.

Every group left thoroughly terrified—but in a good way. No two tours were exactly alike. It would make for a great boost in interest as the attendees compared notes.

Around midnight, when I finished the last tour, my feet hurt and my throat was hoarse.

Velma appeared beside me. "Can I make you a cuppa tea, miss?"

"Thank you, Velma. I'll run upstairs and get into my pajamas, and then take my tea in the drawing room." Back in my room—the second-floor blue room which had been one of the off-limits to guest areas, I climbed out of my historically accurate tour guide costume and hung it carefully. I would need it for the following night's tours, and I didn't want to have to stitch it or press it again because I'd been careless.

Then I made my way to the drawing room in the base of one of the towers. There was a lovely fire crackling in there, and the thought of putting my feet up in front of welcoming flames while I sipped a cup of Velma's signature chamomile, lavender, and valerian tea was exactly what I needed.

After the tea worked its magic, I stumbled sleepily

back to the blue room. Even though the bed-and-breakfast hadn't worked out, leaving the burgundy room available for the tour was still the best financial decision for the manor. It commanded the most interest for many different reasons, and the cobalt door-knobbed room suited me so much more.

With a long and satisfied sigh, I climbed into the enormous four-poster bed with its hand-carved wooden canopy and instantly tumbled into deep and dreamless sleep.

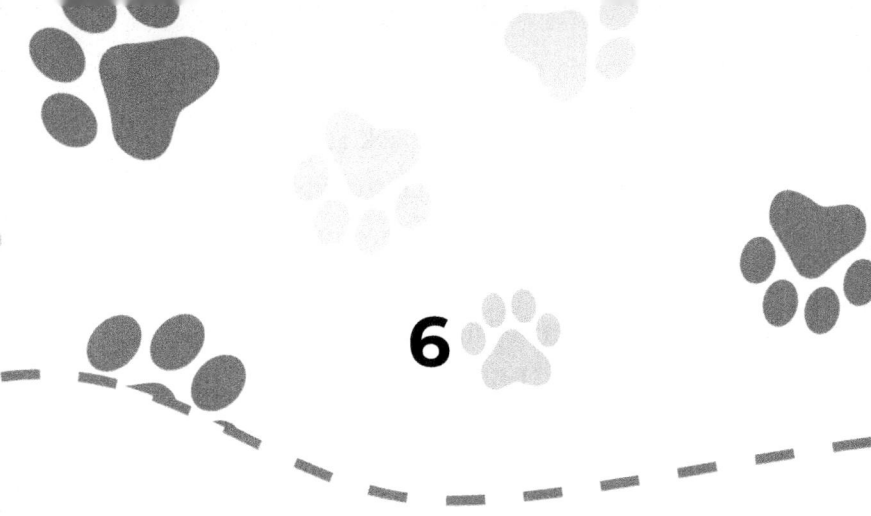

6

Rolling out of my bed in the manor with a smile on my face was a brand-new experience, and I noticed the distinct absence of the weight of dread caused by another day of a dwindling bank account. I opened the thick floor-to-ceiling blue velvet drapes and practically pranced into the bathroom to wash my face and smile at my reflection in the cerulean-trimmed mirror.

"It worked," I crooned gleefully. "The haunted mansion tours are a success, and I'm going to be able to keep this amazing estate." I dried my face and scraped my naturally curly raven locks into a messy bun.

Before I turned away from the mirror, I smiled at

the nearly bare face staring back at me. Not that long ago, I would spend hours flat ironing the curls away in an attempt to erase any trace of my Midwestern, unrefined appearance and then spent another hour on perfecting my makeup application. Not anymore.

For so long, I believed my career in New York had given me the success I longed for when I left the pig farm in Iowa behind. Now I had a different perspective. Living in New York City had changed me in ways I'd never imagined. I had gotten so wrapped up in the hustle and bustle, and trying to keep up with society's pressures, I practically erased the real me.

Now, standing in an actual mansion in Maine, the real Sydney Coleman was reappearing. I didn't have to change who I was to be successful. Sure, I had to take some risks, and live with earthbound spirits—

If there was a sound more terrifying than the shocked scream of a ghost, then I had yet to hear it. My heart stuttered as fear filled me.

Racing down the imperial staircase, I took the steps two at a time as I called out to my otherworldly roommates. "Velma? Is that you? Sir Bogart, what's going on?"

He appeared beside me in the grand foyer as we both hurried toward the back of the manor and the door to the garden. Velma intercepted us, weeping into her hands.

I tried to comfort her, but my hand just disappeared into her energy. "Velma, what's wrong? Why did you scream?"

She whimpered and nodded, too upset to speak. Her ethereal finger pointed at the mudroom and flickered in and out of existence as her tears continued.

Walking past, I froze in my tracks, unable to process the scene before my eyes. My throat tightened and my stomach lurched. No rational thought congealed in my mind. It was blank in shock as I tried to process the scene in front of me.

Sir Bogart sighed harshly. "Women. Bah! You can always count on the fairer sex to overreact." He passed through me and stopped short. "Why is there a strange human sleeping on the floor of our utility room?"

My shaky voice returned. "I— I don't think she's—"

He crouched as though stalking prey and cautiously approached the form. Sniffing the air, he poked at the lump with one paw. "Dead, I'm afraid. As dead as the mouse I intercepted last evening."

It was all too much for me. I leaned against the

wall and sank to the floor. My hand shook as I pulled out my phone and dialed 911.

The calm, confident voice of the dispatcher filled my ear, and I took a deep breath. "There's a body. I think dead."

She calmly asked for the address.

I couldn't take my eyes off the figure. "Um, I can't remember right now. It's Moonlight Manor. Just off the highway—"

The dispatcher interrupted and confirmed that she knew the address, and the sheriff would be there shortly. She instructed me not to move the body or touch anything at the crime scene.

After confirming that I was in no immediate danger, she ended the call.

I struggled to get air into my lungs. "How did this happen? Who is—?"

As soon as I asked the question aloud, a memory of the long, shabby mustard-colored coat and the muddy black galoshes rocketed into my brain. And I knew. I knew who it was.

I gasped. "It's Gladys Williams. What is she doing in my house?"

Sir Bogart reclined beside me. "As you well know, she was displeased with your plans for the tours. It's likely she came to sabotage something. Perhaps she's the individual who released the rodent into the estate."

A weak, humorless chuckle escaped. "I'm not sure if you said that to try to cheer me up or not, but you must know that a huge old place like this has plenty of its own rodents."

He smiled wickedly. "Delightful, is it not?"

A fresh, hideous shiver crept down my spine. "If she came to confront me again, or offer some new threat to stop the tours, how did she get all the way through the house with none of us seeing her?"

Sir Bogart was the first to hear the tires on the drive and vanish. I hurried to the front door and waited anxiously on the granite steps, wringing my hands. The closest person I had to an enemy was deceased in my home. After the best grand opening night we could have hoped for. I resisted the urge to squeeze my eyes closed and try to pinch myself awake.

My breath caught in my throat. It wasn't a residual nightmare. No, this was reality, and Gladys, in her mustard-yellow coat, was dead. I shuddered.

The tall, athletic frame of Sheriff Allen climbed out of the cruiser. "Morning, Sydney. Seems like you had a bit more trouble."

She walked toward me, and I nodded sadly.

"Thanks for coming so quickly, Haley—I mean, Sheriff Allen. I just discovered the body. I don't have any idea how she got in."

"She?"

"Yeah. Right after I got off the phone with dispatch. I remembered where I'd seen the coat and boots. I think it's Gladys Williams."

Sheriff Allen shook her head. "That's not good, Miss Coleman."

Something in her tone concerned me, but I tried not to dwell on it. I led her back to the mudroom at the rear of the manor, but I didn't like the way we'd gone from Sydney to Miss Coleman in the blink of an eye.

Sheriff Allen examined the crime scene and confirmed that the victim was Gladys Williams. She called for the coroner then went back to taking photos of the scene.

Finally, she turned to me. "Miss Coleman, may I speak to you in the drawing room?"

I pushed hair back from my face. "Sure. Of course."

We made our way to the drawing room and I asked if she wanted a cup of coffee.

"No, thank you. I'll get straight to the point. There's no sign of forced entry. There's a history of disputes between yourself and Mrs. Williams. I'm afraid I—"

I gasped in shock to hear it aloud. "You don't think I had anything to do with this, do you? I'd never hurt anyone, let alone kill someone."

"I have to keep my personal feelings out of my investigations, Miss Coleman. I'm placing you under arrest on suspicion of murder. If you're innocent, you'll be cleared and released as soon as possible."

My mouth twisted, and my stomach churned. Arrested? Just like that? Even if I had suspected I might be questioned, I hadn't expected to be escorted from my home and placed in custody.

Bail. I could make bail. If I could make bail, then I could still conduct tours, couldn't I? Then I slumped forward with a grimace. My balance didn't support being loaned a large sum of money to get out. Surely they had different rules for bail loans. Didn't they? I swallowed back a rush of bile. It wouldn't do to puke on Sheriff Allen's freshly-shined shoes.

The entire world seemed to stop spinning, and Sir Bogart even attempted to prevent our exit. But he couldn't stop the sheriff now that she'd decided I should be arrested.

As we moved through the manor, I tried desperately to hang on to my composure. "Sheriff Allen, may I please change out of my pajamas? And I need to call Frannie to see if she can cover the tours for me tonight."

Sheriff Allen crossed her arms and chewed the inside of her cheek as she considered my request. "I can certainly give you a chance to get changed, Miss Coleman. However, there won't be any more tours. The mansion is a crime scene now. We can't have people traipsing through, destroying evidence. You'll have to cancel the remaining tours and I would assume refund any monies you collected. But that's between you and your ticket holders. You've got five minutes to get changed."

Bogey was already in the blue room when I arrived upstairs.

"Please allow me to speak to Haley," he said. "Perhaps I can talk sense into her. She must know you could not be responsible for such an atrocity. Gladys Williams possessed a list of enemies longer than my tail. No living soul would believe you were capable of such malice. Shall Norman and I detain her?"

My eyes widened. "No. If we do anything aggressive, it will only make us—me—look more guilty. The best option I have is to cooperate. You and Velma and Norman can eavesdrop when the police are here collecting evidence. Maybe you'll overhear something that will help us figure out who actually killed her."

"Perhaps, mistress. It is unfortunate that we had over fifty guests enter and exit our home last night."

He couldn't be more right. It was a large pool of suspects.

I nodded quickly. "I know, Bogey. We can figure this out. I'll call Frannie and ask her to be the go-between. She can deliver messages, and maybe she knows a good lawyer."

Sir Bogart hissed loudly. "You are not guilty of these crimes. It seems unlikely you should need a barrister to defend your innocence."

"I wish it were that easy."

Sheriff Allen shouted up from the main floor, sending her warning all through the house. "Time's up, Miss Coleman."

I descended the broad staircase with shoulders slumped. But the worst was yet to come. As I walked across the polished parquet floor, Sheriff Allen pulled the handcuffs from her belt.

"Please turn around and place your hands behind your back, Miss Coleman."

"Are you serious? We have to do the cuffs, too?" I rasped. "I'll get in your car without trouble, Haley."

Sheriff Allen didn't relent. "Please do as I've asked, Miss Coleman."

Before she clicked the handcuffs onto my wrists, she recited the Miranda rights I'd only read about in books before now. And then, the only sound in the whole of Moonlight Manor was the sound of my wrists being shackled together.

Click.

7

*". . . And clouds vanish from the autumn night sky,
The walls of sweet Blodfyss will live and breathe.
Ages of justice from the heart will seethe.
All who dare to enter with ill intent,
Will relive their crime and death's punishment."*

An ill wind blew through the attic, and Sir Bogart vanished with a warning.

I blinked. Something seemed so familiar about all of this. I looked down at the book and ran my fingers over the words I'd just read aloud. Had I seen this somewhere before? Heard it previously? Maybe it had been in a movie. I frowned. No, that wasn't right. Maybe it was a passage copied from a book—

I closed the volume with a snap. There wasn't time to worry about it. I had to finish decorating and add this lovely old book to the display in the entryway. It would be *perfect* there.

As I placed the book, I had another flash of déjà vu. I chalked it up to my mostly sleepless night and dreams I probably didn't remember. Today was the grand opening, and I was so excited, I could barely keep my eyes closed the night before.

When the doorbell chimed, I somehow knew it would be Frannie—with cupcakes.

Hesitantly, I opened the door and stared in shock. Surely I'd been through this before.

Frannie took in my odd expression and eased past me. Her head swiveled on her neck as she took in all the decorations. "It's really shaping up in here, Sydney."

The discussion continued as we walked toward the kitchen. I felt as though I was reciting lines I'd rehearsed, rather than having a new and unique conversation. She mentioned Craig and the way he said the word *lobstah*. But instead of laughing, I couldn't shake my uneasy feelings.

Once we reached the table, I paused. "Frannie, does it feel like we've done this before?"

"What do you mean? Gossiping over cupcakes? Of course. I'd like to think it's kind of our thing."

Trying to laugh it off, I said something about the latest developments. As we continued to talk about the repairs and hammering. Hammering? Yes. There was something about the garden.

I raced to the mudroom at the rear of the house, but everything was fine. Rodney busily fixed the door, and talked about taking his children costume shopping, yet I still felt strange—as though I moved through scenes in slow motion, already knowing every part.

Frannie had to leave but promised to see me this evening.

Velma and I stretched some additional last-minute cobwebs over the entry, but I performed the task as though in a daze. Every time I passed through the grand entry, I thought I heard voices whispering, watching from the shadows.

After interrogating the ghosts, and confirming they weren't playing tricks on me, I ate some leftover chicken in silence.

Maybe a long soak in the tub would help me clear my head. I lit a few candles in the luxurious en suite in the burgundy room and sank into the steamy waters.

The muscle aches from days of cleaning, lifting, and decorating began to fade. While faces of strangers flashed beneath my drooping eyelids.

A couple in 1800s period garb.

An angry teenage boy.

A child in a character mask.

Did I know them? Had I seen them somewhere before?

So much for a relaxing bath. I pulled myself out of the tub and started the laborious process of donning my authentic wardrobe.

I'd uncovered a trunk full of women's clothing in the attic, and Velma had helped me select a complete outfit.

The first layer consisted of a cotton chemise and silk knee stockings held in place with a garter. I'd learned the hard way how important it was to put on my lace-up ankle boots *before* the corset.

The shirt and hoop skirt came next. On top of all this, I slipped a cotton dress over my head, adjusted the skirt, and pinned one of Beatrix de Haviland's cameo brooches at my throat. Throughout it all, Velma assisted where she could.

The cloak and gloves waited for me downstairs.

Time to check in with the ghostly residents and make a final pass through the manor. Everything had to be perfect. My future—*our future*—at Moonlight Manor depended on it.

As I straightened my bonnet and hoped the old dress I'd found in the attic would hold up, I struggled to ignore the knowing dread in my stomach. I had to be on top of my game. This was the grand opening, and word-of-mouth was everything.

Taking a deep breath, I pushed away all the weird confusing thoughts of déjà vu, and dived into my role as tour guide. I warmed up the crowd with some architectural facts and offered the standard disclaimers.

I was about to ask if everyone was ready to start the tour, but—

There it was. Tires on the gravel, and Frannie arriving late. I'd somehow expected exactly that.

Wow. Maybe it was all of this spooky nonsense taking a toll on my brain.

Waving to Frannie, I led the group inside. The lights flickered and Sir Bogart offered them their first taste of ghostly entertainment. They were impressed, and I felt positive about this venture.

As we walked toward the ballroom, I heard a familiar tune from the piano, and I knew it would be Velma on the bench.

The guests couldn't see her, of course.

I pointed to a sullen teenage boy. "Would you like to walk over to the piano and see if you can figure out how it works?"

His eyes widened with shock, almost as though I'd read his mind. However, he and a couple of the other guests stepped closer, while a woman filmed the piano on her phone.

Weird.

Once again, my mouth seemed to be a step ahead. "Would any of you like a drink?"

Norman stepped into the ballroom with a confused look on his face, balancing a tray of drinks. He passed through the room and the guests clapped. Even the sulking teen had a partial grin.

Next, I took the group upstairs and went through the various bedrooms. When we got to the burgundy room, I leaned down to address a small boy. "If you keep an eye on the bed, the kitty is going to appear any minute."

As if on cue, Sir Bogart appeared, and the child's eyes sparkled with wonder.

How did I know? I couldn't answer that. They hadn't shared any of their plans with me or told me their haunting schemes.

Velma drifted in to whisper in some ears, and I ushered the group through the secret tunnel. Before I opened the double doors to release them, I added one more comment. "Be sure to examine Aphrodite as you leave. I think you'll be surprised at what she's pouring from her jug."

Yep, the water had a blood-red glow in the moonlight. And, once again, I'd known it would. Without being told. Or had I been? What was going on?

Frannie was offering giddy congratulations and apologizing for not being able to come back out in the morning with cupcakes.

I couldn't understand what she was saying. Hadn't we had cupcakes two mornings in a row? Nothing was making sense. I raced inside and called out to the others. "Hey, was anything weird tonight? Did you feel like it maybe happened before?"

The three ghosts shook their heads, and I returned to the granite steps to prepare for the next tour.

I finished the night's tours, but I didn't feel successful. I was off my game. There was an odd sense of foreboding. Yet I couldn't put my finger on the cause as Velma helped me out of my historically accurate clothing.

Taking my special tea up to the blue room, I gulped it down in two swigs and hoped the morning would bring the fresh start I needed.

* * *

A dreamless sleep always concerned me. I never felt quite rested by the end.

A blood-curdling scream rousted me from bed.

As I raced down the stairs toward the sound, a sickening feeling grew inside me.

A body. Velma had discovered—

She couldn't speak. Velma simply cried and pointed. But I already knew what waited in the mudroom. I already knew *who* waited. The knowledge that I already knew chilled me through to my bones.

Trancelike, I picked up the phone and called dispatch. "Good morning. Gladys Williams is dead. Somehow she got into my mudroom, and I've only just discovered her body. Can you please send the sheriff?"

We went through the details, and time seemed to pass in the blink of an eye. The next thing I knew, I was arguing my innocence and begging for a moment to change into street clothes. Sheriff Allen reluctantly agreed.

Upstairs in the blue room, I slipped out of my pajamas and pulled on a heavy sweater. As I sat on the edge of the bed, pushing my feet through the legs of my jeans, a cold hand seemed to grip my shoulder.

Jumping from the bed, I looked behind me, keeping my mouth clenched so my teeth didn't chatter. There were no ghosts in the bedroom. It had felt almost as though the hand reached from the other side of the veil. I shivered. What was I saying?

That wasn't possible. Was it?

I frowned as I zipped my jeans and pushed my feet into some warm boots. The hand hadn't happened before, had it? How could any of it have happened before? What was going on? Why did everything seem so familiar? And who killed Gladys? Maybe I was coming apart at the seams. I thought I'd adjusted to life outside the big city, but maybe living with three ghosts was slowly destroying my sanity.

Rushing into the bathroom, I stared at myself in the cerulean-edged mirror. What if my sanity was already slipping? Maybe I didn't live with ghosts. A wince twisted my face. Maybe I lived all alone, and I'd invented spirits from beyond to make myself feel better. I didn't like to think about it or dwell on the past. Yet . . .

It had happened before . . .

When I was a lonely child suffering from bullying at school, I'd escaped into books. I let them consume me. One time, I stood up at show-and-tell in my fourth-grade class and told everyone that I had a pig named Wilbur and he'd won a medal at the state fair.

The children had laughed mercilessly. The teacher sent me to the principal's office for lying, but the kind man honestly tried to comfort me. He said *Charlotte's Web* had been one of his favorite books too, and it would be great to have a pig like Wilbur. I was mortified to be called out like that. I never wanted to go back to school again.

Maybe I had a breakdown after Lucas dumped me.

Was Frannie even real? I couldn't possibly have invented those delectable caramel-apple cupcakes with cinnamon buttercream frosting. Could I?

No, no, of course not.

And now Sheriff Allen shouted for me from downstairs. It was time to face the music. I had to keep moving forward, didn't I?

Stumbling down the grand staircase, I knew the handcuffs would be waiting. I turned and put my hands behind my back before Sheriff Allen could even ask. The cold metal pressed against my wrist and I heard the first click. I didn't remember hearing the second.

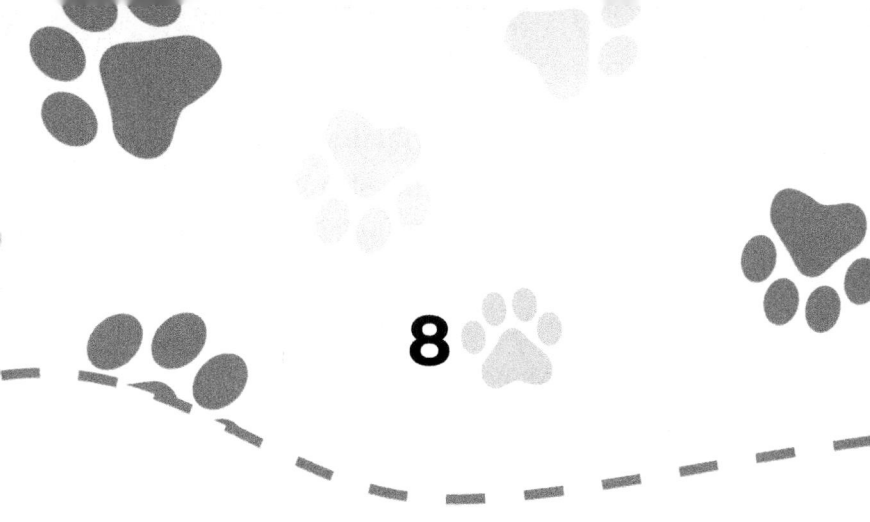

8

". . . The walls of sweet Blodfyss will live and breathe.
Ages of justice from the heart will seethe.
All who dare to enter with ill intent,
Will relive their crime and death's punishment."

The voice of Sir Bogart called from the ether, "You were warned, mistress."

Hold on. I was not imagining it. This definitely happened before.

After I placed the book in the foyer, I called out to the resident feline apparition. "Sir Bogart? Sir Bogart, I have to talk to you."

He appeared on the landing of the imperial staircase with a smug expression. "Is something amiss, mistress?"

"Have you witnessed anything strange?"

Bogey sauntered down the steps with the seductive sway of a runway model, and I finally understood why it was called a catwalk. "What do you mean by strange, mistress? There are a great many odd details about Moonlight Manor."

Hugging my arms around my middle, I inhaled sharply. "Are you experiencing any déjà vu?"

He lifted his proud chin and sniffed. "Are you referring to the recital in the attic?"

I lunged forward eagerly. "Yes. Exactly. I'm sure I read that poem out loud before. And your warning. I heard that before, too."

The fine feline dropped onto his haunches and curled his luxurious tail around his feet. "It is not a poem, mistress. You have recited a spell from the Blodfyss sisters' grimoire. And you did so at your own peril."

"What are you saying? It's just some rhymey little thing. Why would you call it a spell?"

Bogey leapt onto the table and pawed at the book. "Show me the incantation."

Carefully opening the book, I turned the pages until I found what I had thought was a poem. He gazed over the lines, shaking his head more furiously with each stanza.

My eyebrows lowered. "You can read?"

He gazed up at me with immense irritation. "I appear and vanish at will, I speak your human language, and I am, in general, magnificent. Why is it my reading that confounds you?"

"I don't know. Good for you. The more you know . . ."

"The more of what?"

"Don't worry about it. It's this stupid thing I learned in school. So what's the deal with this poem?" Gesturing to the grimoire, I pursed my lips. Was I ready to call it a spell? Well, I was talking to a long-dead ghostly cat, if that was any indication about what I was ready for. "Spell, I meant spell," I added haltingly.

Bogey shrugged—as much as a cat could. "I was not privileged to live during the Blodfyss witches' reign. Legends can be cruelly misinterpreted. The family always maintained that the sisters were good and aided their fellow villagers. However, this particular incantation seems to have a dark twist. The justice of the ages, and death's punishment. Does not sound all rosy and warm." His whiskers quivered. "Or helpful."

I pointed to the line about the walls breathing.

"What if I somehow brought the house to life? Maybe the house killed Gladys."

His large eyes widened and his black slit pupils dilated to near circles. "Gladys is dead?"

Balling my hands into fists, I moaned in frustration. "Yes. No. Not yet. Try to remember. It happens tonight, or maybe tomorrow morning. But at some point Velma screams—"

And suddenly there was a scream.

I spun around and gasped.

Velma had thrown herself from the second floor and crashed against the parquet in silence. Nothing more than the sound of her own shriek to indicate the fall.

We rushed toward her. "Velma? Are you all right?"

She popped into an upright position and covered her mouth as she giggled. "I was practicing a trick for the tours tonight. What do you think?"

Pressing a hand to my chest, I struggled to slow my breathing. "Oh, it's great. Do you remember finding Gladys Williams's body in the mudroom?"

She threw a hand over her mouth and her horrified, shimmering eyes were the only answer I needed.

Sir Bogart paced around the two of us. "So it is only you and I who recall previous events."

I tilted my head. "Are you starting to remember? I'm not sure how many times we've been through this loop. There's no way to keep track, I guess. But I remember things much clearer this time. Should we cancel the tours? Try to make sure things don't happen the way they happened before?"

Sir Bogart stopped and fixed me with an unwavering stare. "I fear that playing with the mechanics of time is not as simple as you would assume. Fate cannot be outsmarted. Hence its name. Instead, we must plan to be more observant. To watch each member of each tour as they pass through our home. Perhaps we will uncover some thread that will lead us to the cause of Mrs. Williams's accident."

I met the feline gaze dead-on. "It wasn't an accident, Bogey. I think I can remember Sheriff Allen arresting me for murder."

His majestic jaw hung open awkwardly.

A clear image of the handcuffs convinced me of the memory. "Yes. Yes, I do remember that. Sheriff Allen arrests me." The doorbell interrupted our discussion.

The ghostly feline turned toward the entrance.

"Oh, that's Frannie. She has cupcakes."

Sir Bogart scoffed. "Hardly the prediction of a world-class psychic."

I scowled at the unsupportive cat. "Well, maybe she'll know what to do."

Despite multiple explanations, and several demonstrations of my prognosticating abilities, Frannie had no memory of living this day before. She assured me that Gladys Williams was alive and well and had purchased a dozen of Heaven Can Bake's finest doughnuts just this morning."

"At least we know she's alive this morning, but sometime between now and then, she dies." My shoulders sagged. "I don't know what to do, Frannie. I'm telling you, that woman ends up dead in my mudroom tomorrow morning. The worst part is, Sheriff Allen thinks I did it, and I'm arrested and trotted off. Or at least I think I'm trotted off. My memory gets a bit fuzzy now and then."

Frannie wiped the buttercream from her mouth. "Nonsense. Haley's a reasonable sheriff. She'll look at all the evidence and figure out what really happened. In all likelihood, Gladys was sneaking in to cause trouble. She hates this idea of your tours, and she probably thought she could throw a monkey wrench in the thing somehow. The woman is old as dirt, Syd. She probably snooped herself into a heart attack. Let's not get worried until the coroner's report is finished. Which I guess will be sometime next week, if Gladys dies tomorrow." Frannie looked at me and shook her head. "It's really weird knowing that someone's going to die. Are you sure you didn't just have a bad dream?"

I threw my arms in the air and shook my head. "I don't. Maybe it was all a bad dream. Maybe the déjà vu is just a side effect of lack of sleep. If I don't pull myself together before the grand opening, I'm gonna sabotage my own venture. Gladys won't have to do anything at all."

She smiled and patted me on the back. "Yes. Pull yourself together. That's the spirit. Midwest sisters unite. I'll be here tonight for the first tour, and I'm sure you'll see these uneasy feelings will be gone by then. Your haunted mansion tours are going to be a fabulous success. I just know it."

If only Frannie had been able to change the future with her optimism.

She showed up for the first tour, which I completed to the great satisfaction of the group, but the knot in my stomach refused to disappear. The second group arrived. There were more young children than I'd remembered. I dashed into the house and warned the ghosts to keep it light and breezy. I didn't want any small children crying their eyes out.

Sir Bogart was especially kind, and Velma allowed

the group to see her for a moment as she gently patted a child's head. None of the guests seemed to have negative reactions to the specters, in fact, it was the opposite.

Another successful group.

I barely remembered walking the third group through. After they left, I hastily checked the mudroom. Nothing. Nobody. Nothing suspicious.

The fourth group arrived—ten teenagers. Sir Bogart must've read my mind. Velma performed her swan dive from the second floor, Norman caused ice crystals to form across the mirror in the lavender bathroom, and Sir Bogart appeared behind them in the burgundy room with a terrifying hiss.

By the time I hustled them down the secret passage and returned to accept Velma's comforting mug of tea, the only thing on my mind was bed.

My brain felt foggy, my thoughts were muddled. As soon as my head hit the pillow . . .

The next thing I knew, there was that blood-curdling scream.

The click of the handcuffs, and—

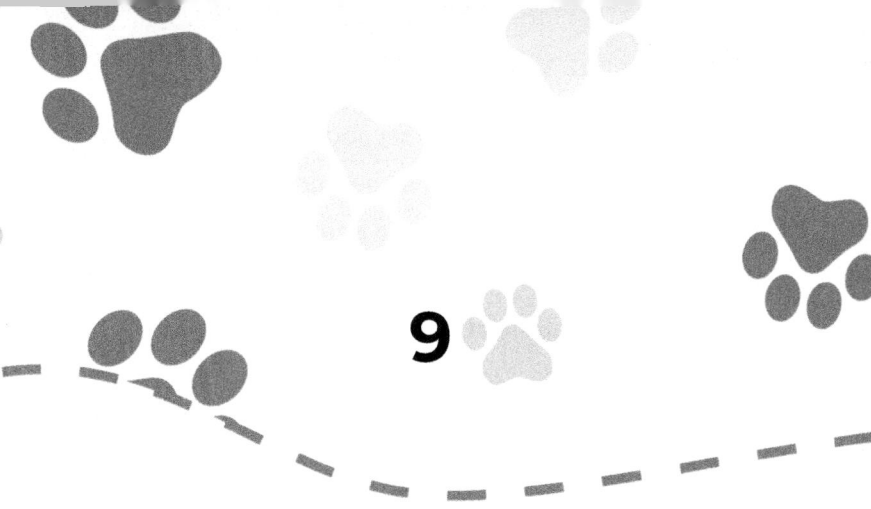

9

Augusta Adams waved to me from the back of the third tour group. The haunted tour hadn't seemed like her thing, so I was somewhat shocked to see her. Or was I? She'd been in the third group before. The shock wasn't new. It must be the memory of the shock . . .

I raised my arms, already tired from the stress of déjà vu and the first two tours. "Follow me into the manor and we'll get started."

The faint pleasure I felt when I saw Augusta in the tour group faded rapidly. She wasn't a fan of the frights, and each and every time I attempted to share a tidbit of historical information about the manor, she instantly—and publicly—corrected me each time we went through this. How many times now?

When we reached the second level and began going through the various bedrooms, I thought perhaps it would be best to stop fighting like a salmon headed upstream and give in. "Augusta, would you like to tell our guests about the various colored door knobs?" I bit back a sigh and stepped slightly to the side.

Augusta launched into a lengthy speech about original glass recipes, rare colors, and the shift from poured glass to blown glass. She rambled on until some of the attendees eyed the exits.

I actually heard one of the teenagers in the audience moan with boredom. When we entered the burgundy room, I overrode her expertise on architecture with my knowledge of the mansion's secrets. The hard worker in me had to try to salvage the tour, even if I was going to be giving it again soon.

Velma drifted in, visible only to me, and whispered in the ears of three of our guests. The fear was palpable. As I opened the secret passage, I gave credit where credit was due. "And the wonderful woman who has been sharing architectural knowledge with us this evening, Augusta Adams, is the one who discovered this passage. The very same route used by the murderer who snuck into Beatrix de Haviland's room."

With that, the guests raced to the escape route and practically ran down the passage.

After I'd given my closing speech and invited them all back, Augusta asked if she could pop into the backyard and take some measurements from the gazebo.

"Are you certain?" Eleven o'clock at night seemed awfully late for taking measurements.

"I want to get started first thing, if you don't mind," she gruffed.

"Of course. I don't have any lights out there yet. Do you have a flashlight? Or maybe your phone?"

She held up a black cylinder. "Yep. Got a flashlight right here. Never travel without it. I won't keep you. I know you've got one more group to go. But I'll see you tomorrow to wrap up the flooring. We'll get a proper roof on there this coming week, and you'll be all set."

At least she'd come prepared. I thanked her profusely and let her guide herself out through the newly replaced rear door.

The final group of the evening was all teenagers. Each of them talking braver than the next. Sir Bogart offered me a telling wink and vanished to inform Velma and Norman of the fun they would soon have. *Again.*

As we entered the home, the teens pushed, shoved, and dared each other to do various things. When Velma took her swan dive over the second floor balustrade to the polished parquet below, the stricken silence was deafening.

I urged them to move forward and investigate the scene. But none of the boastful teens could be bothered. Their bawdy talk diminished to hushed whispers, and by the time we reached the burgundy room, they were all holding hands like a group of first graders on a field trip.

There was barely time to mention the ghost of Beatrix before Velma drifted in and began her whisper campaign.

Girls screamed. Boys screamed. They clutched each other in terror. Secretly, I was most pleased. They were another group full of happy customers, at least they would be when they spoke to others about the tour here. I announced the secret passage, and they were thundering down it before I had the chance to ask them to wait for me at the other end. When I reached the drawing room, it was empty. The former miscreants had raced out of the house and into their cars without a backward glance.

Gazing through the open front doors, I smiled at the blood-red liquid flowing from Aphrodite's jug. It was the best detail to end on and brought the tour in a full circle. If not for the déjà vu, it would be a most triumphant night.

Velma floated next to me, beaming. "We taught them, didn't we, miss?"

I crossed my arms over my period-correct cloak and smiled. "We sure did. I think I'll head up and change into my pajamas. Would you be kind enough to bring me a cup of that amazing tea you brew?"

If ghosts could blush, then that's precisely what Velma did. "Right away, miss." She dipped in a phantom's version of a floating curtsy. Then she vanished, heading for the kitchen, I supposed, and I trudged up to the blue room. Which was purposely not part of the tour because it was my private space.

When I opened the door, I had to double check the cobalt-blue glass handle to make sure I hadn't made a wrong turn. Norman's skills were continually unmatched. The room, which was over a hundred and fifty years old, looked brand new. Every surface gleamed. The bedding smelled like fresh daisies, and every pillow had been perfectly fluffed. Not to mention, there wasn't a shred of filthy clothing on the floor. With all the clutter gone, my room had become a peaceful haven.

Opening the wardrobe, I marveled at what a good

washing could do. Even my yoga pants looked elegant. I chuckled and removed a pair of flannel pajamas from the hanger that Norman had placed them on.

Despite my best efforts, I was having serious trouble struggling out of my attic-found garb. It was finally clear to me why women in the nineteenth century required assistance getting dressed. I could do with a lady's maid right about now.

Velma tapped lightly on the door, and I hobbled over to let her and her tray enter. She swooshed toward the small desk in the corner and set down the tray. "Oh, miss. You should have rung for me. You're likely to sprain something trying to get out of that corset on your own."

I frowned, not recalling having this much trouble getting out of the gown before, but every loop ran together. "I would appreciate any help you can give me."

She instantly went to work loosening hooks and ties, until at last, the hoop skirts and contraptions of torture had been released. Velma even took off my tiny ankle boots and polished them with the corner of her apron.

"You know, Velma, I thought it would be stressful and intrusive to have servants trying to help me at every turn, but you have been absolutely wonderful. I can't imagine managing things around here without you."

She took a deep curtsy and smiled. "I felt the same about living with a human, miss. You've been real decent. To all of us." With that, she took her leave.

I sipped the comforting tea and crawled into my massive bed.

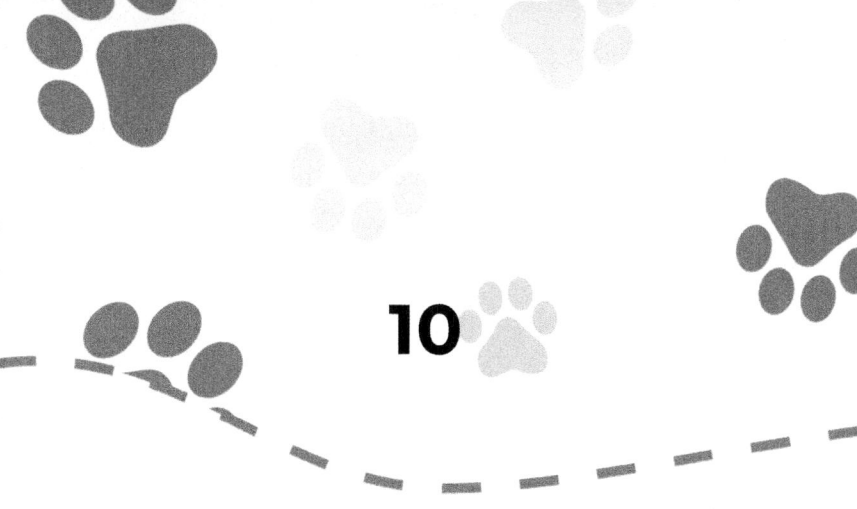

10

One minute the handcuffs clicked into place and the next I found myself, as expected, in the attic reading from the Blodfyss grimoire.

Again.

Still.

This had to be at least the sixth time now, and I was more than a little fed up.

I gritted my teeth. Screaming wouldn't help me right now.

Nope, not today. I was going to beat this thing, fair and square—and no matter what it took.

I headed to the kitchen and called for Sir Bogart.

He popped in and glared at me. "Precisely as you had predicted, mistress."

Breathing a sigh of relief, I pushed brew on the coffeemaker, and sat dejectedly at the table. "So you remember?"

He nodded his proud feline head. "I remember, but I do not understand. You referred to this as a loop? I must admit I have not heard of such a thing. Please explain."

After a slow exhale, I made an attempt. "I'm no quantum physicist, Bogey. The only thing I know about loops like this is from what I've read in books. *Fiction* books. Anyway, something triggers the reset. And then the loop begins again."

He licked the back of his left paw and cleaned what I hoped wasn't mouse fur from his whiskers. "And how many times will this particular loop repeat?"

I stood, poured myself a cup of coffee, and shrugged. "No idea. I think it has something to do with Gladys getting killed. Until Sheriff Allen arrests the right person, I think it'll just keep looping." My gaze narrowed. "Though, maybe the details are slightly different or I notice slightly different details each time. I can't be sure."

He leapt onto the chair opposite me and put his paws on the table as he leaned toward me. "Mistress, Sheriff Allen arrested you, if I remember correctly.

She believes you committed the murder, so what point is there in continuing this loop?" He cocked his head to the side and waited.

"I don't know, Bogey. Haley can't honestly suspect me of murder. How could she? Seems like it was an arrest of convenience. And it looks like the universe agrees. If she made the right arrest, then this whole thing would be over."

He nodded his head. "Then it is up to us. It shall not be the first murder we have solved, mistress."

I smiled. "True. But we don't have any helpful evidence or eyewitnesses. I wouldn't know where to begin."

"True. True." Bogey scratched his chin with the claws of his right paw. "Perhaps we are going about this all wrong. I may have misspoken regarding the fabric of time. If you cancel the tours, we may change the outcome of the evening."

"Maybe. But if we cancel the tours, we'll have to refund the money. We kind of need the money, and I only want to do that as a last resort."

He glared to let me know how much he didn't agree with my decision.

I made a face. "Maybe I'll change my mind at loop ten or so."

Sir Bogart tilted his head from side to side. "At

first blush, that seems a correct course of action. However, if you proceed as planned, and Sheriff Allen arrests you for murder, we will have to cancel all the tours, and come up with yet another plan to save the manor."

I couldn't argue with that. Plus, he had the wisdom of the ages on his side. After all, he'd been a ghost for many years longer than I'd been alive. He certainly knew more about magic than I did. I was simply making major decisions based on my need for income. The best thing I could do would be to try something different than I'd done up to this point.

"If you want to change what you get out of life, change what you're putting in," I murmured.

"What was that?" Sir Bogart asked.

"I said I'm willing to give it a try. This might be the fourth or fifth or sixth time we've been through the loop. I don't think changing the order of the evening is something we tried on previous loops. So let's give it a shot."

Pulling out the list of ticket holders, I emailed and called every contact, to let them know about the unexpected cancellation. I blamed a plumbing issue in the aged house. While untrue, nobody wanted to visit a location without bathrooms. So I offered them the choice between tickets for another night or a refund. I hoped that most people would accept tickets for an alternate date, and most of them did.

Once we'd taken care of notifying the guests, I called a meeting of the manor inhabitants. The four of us went over everything we knew about the guests or remembered from the tours. The bad news was there had only been a couple of familiar faces. However, there was some good news. Norman was now experiencing déjà vu. Velma still seemed shocked by it all. So now, three quarters of the team were remembering looping. I didn't know exactly what that would buy us, but at least I was no longer alone.

I made a quick trip in to town to update Frannie with a couple of menu changes. And to tell her face-to-face why we had to cancel the tour. It wasn't the kind of thing I wanted to tell her over the phone.

When I quietly mentioned that we hoped to prevent the death of Gladys Williams, a strange expression gripped her features. Her hands shook, and she set her coffee mug on the table between us. "Wait. Did you tell me this before?"

My heart almost leapt out of my chest, and I clutched my coffee mug so tightly I thought it might crack. "Yes. I think it was the second loop. You were at my house, and we were having cupcakes and coffee. You thought I was crazy."

She slipped her hands around her mug and gripped it for comfort. "I think I remember that, Syd. I'm sorry I didn't believe you."

"Don't worry about it. I'm still not sure I believe it myself. But Bogey and Norman are remembering now, too. Canceling the tours for tonight may be the way to fix everything. We canceled the tours so no one comes to the house, and that means no one has a chance to kill Gladys. Hopefully, that's the way to end the loop."

Frannie nodded as though discussing repeating time loops was normal bakery conversation. She was nearly as chill as when I told her about the ghosts. Her unflappable nature continually surprised me. How had I lucked into somebody like Frannie?

She drummed her fingers on the surface in front of her. "You know, not that anyone would miss her. She's a terrible woman who has had a run-in with just about everyone in town. I'm not saying she deserved to die, but I don't think Sheriff Allen should be looking at you as the only suspect."

Sipping my coffee, I nodded in agreement, but I wasn't sure how to respond.

Frannie reached across the table and patted my

hand. "Do you want me to come out to the manor and stay with you tonight? Between the two of us, maybe we can change things."

I felt like an idiot for not thinking of that sooner. "Would you? That would be two changes to the pattern. Plus, then I'd have an alibi."

She chuckled, and her brown eyes sparkled. "Well, this is exciting. I've never been an alibi before. Is there a class? Some kind of official certification? Maybe a permit from the city?"

Her lighthearted teasing made me smile. "You're a great friend, Frannie."

She brushed my compliment away with a wave of her hand. "Nonsense. You'd do the same for me. I mean if I lived with ghosts and was caught in a murderous time loop . . ."

The laughter that shook my shoulders eased the tension, and I felt hope for the first time in—I couldn't say how long.

11

As I drove Blue Bell back to Moonlight Manor, the sense of dread melted away. I'd gladly take the hit in income if it meant breaking the loop once and for all. Things were going to be different this time. We had taken action, and if we could change the pattern, then it made total sense that we could change the outcome. It was a breeze to complete my checklist. How hard could it be? Heaven only knows how many times I'd finished it.

And I still had plenty of time left in the day before I had to get myself ready to play world's best tour guide...

Wait.

No tours tonight.

How could I forget?

Great. My forgetfulness had to be a result of going through the loop again and again. How bad would it get before we were able to move on? My heart twisted, and my mood threatened to dip. But I pushed it all away. No negativity allowed.

I'd simply keep myself busy until Frannie showed up. I could walk the entire perimeter of Moonlight Manor and give the exterior a good once-over. The exercise would have a great mood-boosting benefit, too, so I marched out of the manor without delay.

As I ran my fingers along the rusticated granite, it occurred to me I'd never actually done this on the exterior of my manor. It was a little intimidating to stand in the shadow of such a massive mansion.

There hadn't been enough money in the budget to get the grounds manicured, but for our purposes now, the wild overgrowth, the dead leaves, and the tree limbs scratching at the windows seemed appropriate for the new venture.

The bones of the new gazebo were in sight, but something beyond that structure caught my eye. One of the disrepair structures, probably, but I wasn't sure. I really hadn't spent any time on the outlying property of my home. My cash purchase hadn't required a lot of structure inspections, and I hadn't demanded them.

Patting one of the pillars as I passed the gazebo, I wondered if we'd get to have our Halloween feast. If Sir Bogart and I couldn't solve this murder, it would be curtains for the haunted tours.

I passed the charred remains of what was most likely the old chicken coop; the one the Williamses had supposedly set fire to at one time. The wilderness had mostly reclaimed it, although two scorched but sturdy support timbers remained. Maybe I should rebuild it and raise my own chickens for eggs. I tipped my head. Could Velma leave the manor? If so, maybe Velma could help me with them. She would probably know more about raising chickens at Moonlight Manor than I did. Wait . . . Were chickens afraid of ghosts?

The wandering thought brought a chuckle. My farm girl roots were certainly showing now. One minute I could barely meet the needs of a demanding ghost cat, and the next I was planning for a brood of egg-laying hens. Go figure.

The building that caught my eye was about a hundred yards ahead, and appeared sturdy, despite its dilapidated exterior. I scowled, trying to make out what I was looking at. Was it some kind of cabin? Maybe the land steward's housing from long ago?

During my initial tour of the property, Mia Jones

had indicated that all the outbuildings were in disrepair, and the main house had survived the ages because of its superior craftsmanship and hearty stone construction. Her words certainly seemed true to life.

I stumbled on a thick root growing across the lightly worn path I followed. A small stove pipe pierced through the sharply angled roof of the shack and as I approached, I could've sworn I saw a puff of smoke.

This definitely hadn't occurred in the previous loops, and I had no lingering feelings of déjà vu to lead me to believe it had. "Is someone there? You're trespassing on Moonlight Manor property. I'll give you two minutes to get off my land or I'm calling the sheriff."

The crooked door flew open and Gladys Williams came at me, cane raised.

Screaming, my instincts took over as she barreled forward. I'd worked with a few unbroken horses during my time in the Future Farmers of America back in Iowa. A quick dodge out of harm's way, and I swung my arms around, grabbing the cane firmly in two hands. I yanked the walking stick from my psychotic neighbor and threatened her with her own weapon before I even knew what I'd done.

"What are you doing, Gladys? Why are you hiding in there?" I yelled. "How many times do you have to be kicked off this land before you take it seriously?"

Her eyes were wild, and her words made little sense. "No witch is gonna steal my land. You may have put a spell on the rest of Misty Meadows, but I got a special talisman. You can't hex me."

I gaped at her. "What are you talking about?"

She lunged for her cane, but I pulled it away and then moved it firmly to the center of her chest. The fire in her eyes cooled, but she remained extremely agitated, flapping her arms and huffing.

I jerked my head back and to the side. "Gladys, I've told you, Augusta Adams has told you, and most importantly, Sheriff Allen has told you, that row of pine trees is the property line, and the shack you're hiding in is on *my* side. There is a huge granite pillar on that corner and if you walk to the other end of the property, there's another one. Those are my boundary stones. What are you doing in this shack?"

She backed toward the entrance of the shack and snarled like a cornered animal. "You keep away. You keep your potions and your spells to yourself. What I do in my home is my business."

Did she just call this shack her home? I suddenly became far more concerned with her sanity than any nonsense about property disputes. What trouble was she planning for Moonlight Manor?

I raised my hands slowly. "Gladys, move away from the door. I need to see what's going on in here."

The New York City girl in me wondered if she was cooking up some illegal drugs on my property, but I'd have to check to be sure. I couldn't let her go through with whatever she had planned.

Gladys wedged herself in her doorframe, and she wouldn't budge. I tapped her threateningly with the walking stick. Not hard enough to injure her, but enough to let her know I meant business. She leapt at me with the speed of a creature half her age.

Again, survival took over, and I swung the cane in defense.

The thick piece of wood connected with a thud against her side.

I knocked Gladys sideways, and she hit the ground. She didn't move.

Panic gripped my chest, and sharp pain shot through me. No. No. No! Did I just kill Gladys Williams?

It was all true.

Sheriff Allen had been right.

My mind spun in confused and terrified circles. Pulling my cell from my pocket, I stared at the screen.

I was a murderer. I'd murdered someone. Tears streamed down my face and my vision blurred. I dropped the walking stick and wiped my tear-streaked face.

It was self-defense. Sheriff Allen would understand. I didn't mean to hurt Gladys. I pressed and held nine, and a moan escaped from the body on the ground.

I dropped to my knees. "You're alive? You're alive!" Relief swirled with hideous sickness in my stomach. And I took several deep breaths as I knelt next to her.

She didn't answer, but a shuddering sigh slipped from her.

"Gladys? Gladys, can you hear me?"

I didn't know if it would be safe to move her, and as I weighed my options, she rolled onto her back and stared up at me with a mixture of respect, fear, and malice.

"Typical witch," she snapped.

I frowned. "Hey, I didn't mean to hurt you. You lunged at me like a wild animal. I was only defending myself."

"The apple doesn't fall far from the tree on Blodfyss Estate," she hissed.

I stared at her, trying to figure out how to get her

to give in. This woman was utterly hopeless. I climbed to my feet, left her where she was, and opened the door of the shack. Any ill will I felt toward Gladys Williams melted as soon as my eyes adjusted to the dim interior.

A cot with a thin blanket.

A camping stove and a single pot.

A small wood-burning fireplace in the corner with a little pile of split wood.

A meager stack of canned goods.

"Gladys, do you—"

* * *

I came to in a wheelbarrow next to the gazebo. A knot the size of a golf ball throbbed on the back of my head. However, the origins of my current predicament were foggy at best.

What was I doing outside? How did I get into a handcart? My face pinched as I tried to sort through my bits of memories. It wasn't a part of the looping, was it?

It took three attempts before I could extract myself from the wheelbarrow. I stumbled into the house to get some ice for my head.

Sitting in the corner of the kitchen, my elbows on

the table and a bag of frozen peas pressed to the back of my skull, I tried to retrace my steps. The last thing I remembered was heading outside to walk the perimeter of the house.

Maybe I went to look at the restoration work on the gazebo and tripped over some lumber or a stray tool. I could've hit the back of my head when I fell into the wheelbarrow. But where did the wheelbarrow come from? Something about Gladys? I couldn't be sure.

Norman appeared, and, when he saw my predicament, became agitated. "What's happened, madam? Are you unwell?"

I lifted my aching head and sighed. "Norman, do you remember this from any of the previous loops?"

He shook his ghostly head. "No, madam. I feel certain this incident is brand new."

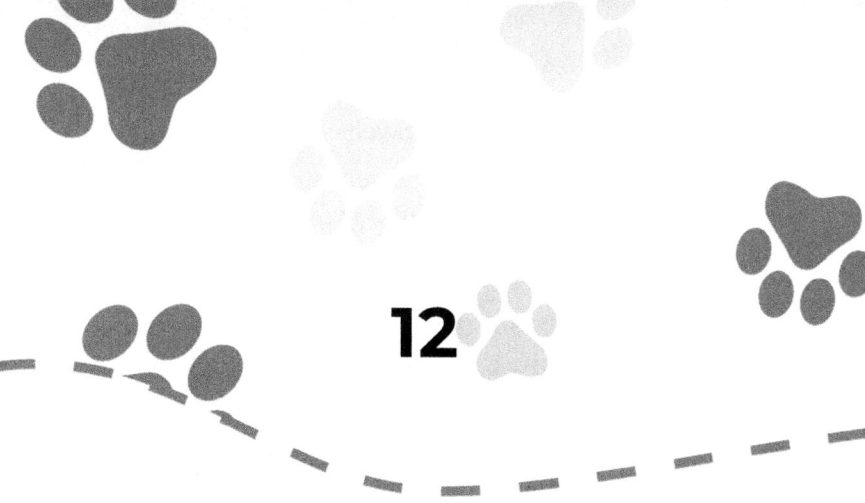

12

If there was any doubt to my or Norman's memories, Sir Bogart arrived to set things straight. "Perhaps Clotho, Lachesis, and Atropos were angered when you picked at the threads of their weave, mistress."

The names he mentioned didn't immediately bring faces to mind, and I wondered how hard I had hit my head. Was it worth a trip to the emergency room? Probably one I couldn't afford. That took care of that idea.

Instead, I slowly walked across the kitchen and returned the frozen peas to their home. "What do you mean?" I winced as I gently rubbed the back of my head.

"Neither you, I, nor Norman remember such an

incident in our previous travels through the day's events. We may regret canceling the tours and tempting the wrath of the three sisters."

"The Blodfyss sisters?"

Sir Bogart lifted his chin and slowly lowered to his haunches. His tail swept behind him, creating a "J" and then a reverse "J," as it twitched from one side to the other. "Oddly, I had not made that connection. But it is worth noting. Of the fates, there were three, and some link to the trio of Blodfyss sisters there may be."

"All I can say is, I'm glad I don't have to lead those tours tonight. My head is beating like a drum. Maybe I should call Frannie and tell her not to worry about coming out."

Norman gasped, and Bogey leapt to the counter. He trained his bright eyes on me. "Mistress, it is unwise to draw another soul into this perplexing conundrum."

"Why? Nothing happened to Frannie in any of the previous loops, and she came to the first tour, anyway. She was here in every loop."

Sir Bogart shook his majestic head and scoffed. "No harm came to your fair head on previous loops, either."

I pursed my lips as I considered his words. "Good point. I'm calling her now."

As the phone rang through, I toyed with the idea of telling her about my run in with Gladys Williams, but something told me that secret was best kept. "Hey, Frannie. I had a minor accident in the backyard and bumped my head."

In an instant, she was ready to close the bakery and race to my aid.

"No. I'm fine, Frannie. Just a lump, and I'm already feeling a bit better, too." At least that much was true. "Nothing some ice and rest won't fix. I was calling to tell you there's no need to come out. I'm just going to turn in early and hope that tomorrow is a new day. And by new day, I mean one that doesn't start with that bone-chilling scream."

She tsked. "Sydney, the absolute worst thing to do after receiving a bump on the head is go to sleep. I'll come out to the manor and there's nothing you can say to change my mind."

"I don't want anything to happen to you, Frannie. Bogey's worried that we may have angered the Fates by trying to change things in the loop."

"Look, a tough Midwestern girl isn't afraid of the Fates, and now I have two reasons to keep you company. I'll keep you awake until any head-trauma-related danger passes, and I can still be your alibi."

The call ended, and I looked to Norman and shrugged helplessly. "There's no stopping Frannie. She's coming out to the manor, and that's that."

Sir Bogart bounded from the kitchen with a scoff. "Yet another of my warnings you have ignored."

Bogey was right. He warned me about the grimoire and I'd ignored him. My own actions may have been the thing that put this entire sequence of events in motion. I walked to the foyer, snatched the grimoire from the walnut table, and made my way up to the attic.

With as wobbly as I still felt, it was slow going, and I had to keep one hand on the railing at all times, but eventually I made it to the top, and—

The light was dim in the uppermost floor as the sun slipped away. How long had I been out? Wow. This tour idea was quickly ending up as my worst yet.

Opening the old trunk where I had originally discovered the grimoire, I dropped it back in. Before I could close the trunk, some trick of light illuminated a sphere in a dark corner of the trunk itself.

Bending down, I gripped the glass orb and lifted it into the diminishing light. As the pinkish-purple setting sun hit the curved surface, the entire globe seemed to glow from within. For a moment I thought I saw Frannie arriving. When she exited her vehicle, she had a bag of takeout from Nanita's, the Mexican place on Main Street.

My stomach growled, and I shook my head. Weird.

The globe would make a suitable replacement for the book on the display, so I closed the trunk. Then I eased my way back down to the main floor and rearranged the items on the entry table. The glass ball wasn't as impressive as the large grimoire, but if it could stop the time loop from repeating, I didn't much care what it looked like.

Events had been changed. The grimoire was safely back in the attic, and—

Gravel crunching under tires.

I opened the front door and stepped onto the terrace.

Hooray. It was Frannie.

My joy turned to icy fear when she exited the vehicle carrying a to-go bag from Nanita's.

My thoughts ground to a halt, and it took a moment to collect them.

Frannie stopped short between the stone stops and the fountain. "You okay?"

Despite my head injury, I hurried down the steps

and called out. "Frannie, are you sure we didn't do this before? Somehow, I knew you were going to bring that food."

She shrugged her shoulders and handed me the bag. "Don't stress out. We're all a little psychic every now and then. You know me well enough to know I generally arrive with food, and there aren't a lot of options this time of day. Just chalk it up to your intuition and don't read too much into it."

Easy for her to say. She hadn't been stuck in a time loop for who-knew-how-many days. When we walked into the foyer, I eyed the glass sphere with suspicion.

Frannie followed my gaze. "What happened to the big book? If you ask me, I think that looked a lot better than the crystal ball."

"Crystal ball? Like a fortuneteller's crystal ball?" More witchy paraphernalia. How did I keep grabbing creepy stuff like that?

She shrugged. "Sure. They're a dime a dozen this time a year. Where did you grab that one? The five-and-dime?"

I took a step away from the table and shook my head. "I found it in the attic. When I looked into it, I saw you arriving with this food."

Frannie's uproarious laughter caught me off

guard. "Oh, I needed that." She pressed a hand to her stomach and wiped tears of laughter from the corners of her eyes. "I gotta hand it to you, Syd. You are really committed to this haunted mansion thing. Now, let's forget about crystal balls and dig into these delicious street tacos. I'll get the plates. You have a seat at the table and take it easy."

I didn't have the courage to argue or explain I wasn't kidding about the crystal ball in the magic trunk of witching things. It lit up as though it wanted me to choose it as the replacement. Hadn't it? My stomach twisted in knots and I worried I'd dropped something worse in place of the grimoire.

We moved to the kitchen and dished up the food. No sooner had I dug into the chips and guacamole than Bogey appeared. "Mistress, there is an object that concerns me in the foyer."

My shoulders drooped. I already knew, but I didn't want to talk about it. "Don't start, Bogey. My head is throbbing and I just want to get through this night and wake up tomorrow with no dead body in the mudroom. After that, you can lecture me all you want."

He vanished, mostly. His judgmental eyes stared daggers at me for a few seconds before he completely disappeared from the visual plane.

Frannie smirked. "Sounds like you're having a disagreement with your ghost cat."

"He's unhappy about the crystal ball. I just don't have the energy to argue about this stuff anymore. Can I get you a glass of wine?"

She smiled. "Yes. But only for me. It's not a great idea to drink alcohol when you have a concussion."

I exhaled loudly. *No sleep. No wine.* "In that case, I think this day is going to be the death of me."

"Technically, this day is going to be the death of Gladys Williams, unless you've fooled fate."

There was no stopping the laughter. I knew it was wrong to joke about such a tragedy, but exhaustion and this blasted time loop had gotten the better of me. I let the laughter take me, temporarily erasing the worry over the various looming disasters, and enjoyed an evening with my best friend.

13

The hours drifted away as Frannie and I played canasta, a game we both remembered from our youths on our respective farms. After she'd finished the bottle of wine, she felt confident enough to insist on playing poker—to keep me awake, she assured me.

We failed miserably at poker, but the laughter and the camaraderie filled my heart in a way I hadn't experienced for years. It soothed the aching in my soul and the worry about a murder and keeping the lights on.

Good friends were hard to find, and Frannie was my first since New York City. I was extremely grateful that I had her in my life. I covered a yawn.

She squinted her eyes at me. "What was that?"

"Look, I have to get some sleep. The potential for any concussion-related disasters has passed. Thanks for keeping me awake and entertained, though."

She took the plates and glasses to the sink and started to wash up.

"What are you doing?"

"I have to be on my best behavior. I want to be invited back."

"Frannie, I insist you stop washing dishes this instant. You're a guest in my home and a friend who already does way too much for me as it is. Seriously, there's no need for you to earn your keep."

She finished rinsing her wineglass and set it on the drying rack. "Well, if you put it that way."

Frannie helped me upstairs, and after offering her the choice of any of the other sixteen bedrooms, I gave up. She insisted that as my official alibi, her only option was to sleep on the couch in the blue room.

Such a sleek modern sofa was completely out of place, but it was the first actual piece of furniture I bought with my own money. I should probably have gotten rid of it but I kept it around for sentimental reasons. "Tell you what, I'll make a deal with you. If you let me take the couch this time, I promise you can have it for the next sleepover. Sound good?"

There was no response.

I stopped tucking the sheets around the buttery cream-colored leather sofa and turned toward the four poster bed. Frannie had collapsed onto the brocade duvet and instantly fallen asleep—with a smile on her face.

After pulling the covers over her, I climbed under the blankets on the sofa. I hadn't slept here since the first couple of terrifying nights in the manor. Once I discovered the true secrets of Moonlight Manor, I found it quite easy to sleep in the enormous king-sized creation. I supposed the same was true for Frannie.

Stretching my arms over my head, I yawned loudly. I expected Frannie to make some kind of smart remark about my lazy sleep in. Yet, when I opened my eyes, the intricate details of the hand-carved wooden canopy loomed overhead.

Wait . . .

I sat up with a start and scanned the room. There were no sheets or blankets on the sofa, and I was in the bed. In fact, there was no evidence there had been anyone other than me in the room. *Oh no.* Had everything reset?

Touching the back of my head, I flinched. The tender spot where I bumped it still hurt. So some things hadn't changed, and it meant we were still *after* waking in the wheelbarrow.

I threw my covers back, grabbed my cell off the nightstand, and put the call on speaker as I headed downstairs. Would there be any evidence of last night's hangout?

Frannie's upbeat voice came over the speaker. "How's my favorite haunted mansion tour guide?"

"I'm all right. What time did you leave?"

"Leave, from where? I pretty much left my house at the usual time this morning. I was running about five minutes late, but I got the bakery open on schedule, so my customers were none the wiser. Why do you ask?"

My head spun, and it had nothing to do with yesterday's concussion. "Hold on. Are you telling me you don't remember anything about being at my house last night?"

Frannie was oddly silent. I waited patiently, hoping some memory would trickle through. At long last, a strangled cry echoed from my phone.

"Do you remember? Wine. Canasta. Please tell me you remember."

Her voice was soft and shaky. "Maybe, but it

must've been a dream. How did I get home? I would never drive in that condition."

"I can't explain it. I've got to check on something in the—"

At that exact moment, Velma's blood-curdling scream ripped through the manor.

Unceremoniously ending the call, I raced toward the mudroom. Velma hovered outside, but she wasn't crying. Her glowing features showed nothing but confusion peppered with fear.

No, no, no, please, no. Not again. We changed so much.

I attempted to grab her shoulders, but of course my hands went straight through. "Oh no. Is it Gladys Williams? Did you find a body in the mudroom?"

She nodded and vanished from my sight.

"Bogey. Norman. It happened again." I peeked around the corner, just for my edification, but the body clothed in a shabby, mustard-colored coat and galoshes was still there.

The butler and the boss cat appeared in a flash.

"It happened again. Nothing we did changed the outcome. Gladys is still dead. And we all know I'll be the prime suspect. Plus, somehow Frannie was transported home in the middle of the night."

Bogart circled the body, sniffed the air, and sighed

morosely. "I feel we cannot defeat the sisters, neither those of fate nor those who wove the clever spell into the grimoire."

"The grimoire." Without waiting for anyone else to get on board, I ran to the entryway. There, on the round walnut table, lay the grimoire. The crystal ball from yesterday's discovery was gone. What? How could this be? I covered my face in my hands and considered collapsing to the floor. But I couldn't. No, I had to forge the way ahead, so I dropped my hands and lifted my face.

Norman and Bogey were immediately at my side.

I pointed to the large leather-bound tome and nearly cried. "How? I put it in the trunk. I carried it up to the attic, put in the trunk, took the crystal ball, and I closed the trunk. How could this happen?"

Norman shook his head. "I fear I have nothing to add to this discussion, madam. I should be on my way to check on Velma. Perhaps she remembers, and then four heads will certainly be better than three."

Nodding, I walked toward the imperial staircase and took a seat on the first riser. "Bogey, canceling the tours didn't work. What do we do now?"

Bogey and I sat in silence. He reclined a step above me while I perched on the bottom step, rocking back and forth to comfort my frayed nerves.

Norman returned with Velma in tow and brought us a brief flash of cheerful news. "Velma remembers, madam. Now we may all work together to seek an alternate solution to this time-loop dilemma."

"What do you remember?"

Velma tucked her gray-blonde hair under her bonnet and adjusted her apron. "I ain't exactly sure, miss. When I were headed to the mudroom this morning. There was a part of me that already knew what I'd find."

"So why did you scream?"

"Sorry, miss." She bobbed her head and curtsied. "Even though I were expecting it. Well, it still gave me a fright."

"Yeah, I imagine it did." Smiling, I nodded my head. "So, you sensed you'd done it before, and you remembered the body. Did you know it was going to be Gladys?"

"Not at first, miss. But as soon as I saw her, it all came back. And I knew you'd be running down. That part came back to me too."

We exchanged knowing glances. Velma's story was quite similar to all of ours.

"Let's take another look at the grimoire. Canceling the tours absolutely didn't change anything, maybe there's a clue in the poem—"

Sir Bogart loudly cleared his throat. "Spell."

"Yes. You're absolutely correct. Spell." A sudden, and hopefully brilliant, thought flashed into my head. "Or maybe there's a different spell. One that would end this loop."

Sir Bogart leapt onto the circular table and sat firmly on the book. "That is not how magic works, mistress. You lit a fuse on this ball of energy when you read the words aloud, and until that flame is satisfied, it will continue to exist in the world. You must discern how to satisfy the spark. Until we do that, I fear this loop will continue for all of us."

"That is totally unacceptable." I marched back to the stairs and returned to rocking back and forth. "We found this spell easy enough. There must be some other spell that can counter the first."

"Miss, I know I don't remember as many loops as the rest, but I have an idea."

"Please, Velma. All ideas are welcome."

Velma clasped her hands in front of herself. "Well, if we can't change the thing for Mrs. Williams, then maybe it's her time. My dear mother used to say, there ain't none fit enough to outrun death's sickle."

I kept rocking back and forth. "Your mother had a good point. I would agree with her but outrunning the grim reaper's sickle isn't exactly the issue. The problem is, when we call to report the death, Sheriff Allen arrests me for the murder. I didn't do it, and that's what we're trying to avoid. After the handcuffs click, everything resets."

Velma and Norman exchanged worried glances, then she turned back to me, smiling bright as the sun. "Not to worry. Seems like all you got to do then is solve this murder, miss. We done it before. You figured out who killed sweet Miss de Haviland, when there weren't no one alive to help you."

I took a deep breath and held it. "Well, Sir Bogart and I discussed that several loops ago, but we didn't pursue it. Old Gladys has so many enemies, we weren't sure we could narrow it down."

Velma bobbed her head. "Yes, miss. That were true. But it can't hurt to try, could it?"

14

Standing abruptly, I brushed my hands together and plastered a grin on my face. "You know what? You're right. It absolutely can't hurt to try to investigate. What do you say, team? Are you willing to solve another murder with me?"

Norman bowed deeply. "It would be my honor, madam."

Gazing down at Sir Bogart, I crossed my arms. "Well, that's three out of four. What about you, Bogey?"

He sniffed haughtily and cleaned his whiskers. "If it will end this infernal looping, I shall join in the effort."

"Changing details doesn't seem to work."

His ears swiveled toward me. "Too true. Then let's get on with it, shall we?"

I worried my next suggestion would be met with strong resistance. "In that case, I'm going to recommend that we don't call the sheriff."

Velma's eyes widened, but no one disagreed.

I gestured toward the general direction of the mudroom, trying not to think of the deceased. "For the record, I'm not exactly comfortable with it either, but I'm thinking that if the goal is to solve the murder on our own, we'll have more time if we put off making the call. In the previous loops, as soon as Sheriff Allen arrives, she puts me in the handcuffs and that resets everything. So if we give ourselves some time to investigate before making the call, maybe we'll get closer to the truth this time. Plus, if all else fails, it seems like the loop resets itself, no matter what we do."

"That sounds real smart, miss." Velma smiled. "How can I help?"

"Follow me." I led the trio of ghosts toward the mudroom, suddenly thankful for my ghostly friends. "Try not to think about what's in there, Velma. I can't touch anything, or my fingerprints will absolutely be all over the crime scene. But the three of you can search through everything without leaving a trace."

Sir Bogart inhaled sharply. "That is most ingenious, mistress."

I did a quick imitation of a curtsy and thanked him. Standing well outside the mudroom to keep my fingerprints and—I didn't know, maybe DNA evidence—as far away from the crime scene as possible, I gave instructions to my sleuthing specters.

"Check the body for any type of bruising, or something worse." I stood up on my tiptoes to try to see as they hovered over the mustard yellow coated figure. "In the chest, or anywhere really."

Norman went straight to work. "Are you suggesting a knife wound, or perhaps something caused by a gun, madam?"

"That's right. Why do you ask?"

"I wanted to be clear about the parameters."

Gulping, I tried to push the disturbing images from my head. "Yeah, that sounds good."

Norman searched the body and popped up a few moments later. "Nothing, madam. No blood and no open wound."

I scowled. "How odd."

Velma wrung her hands together, floating over Gladys, while Sir Bogart circled the body, sniffing here and there. "What now, miss?" Velma asked.

"Velma? I hate to ask, but would you be comfortable looking underneath her clothes?"

The apparition of the cook flickered, and she nodded hesitantly. The rest of us waited in silence as Velma allowed her energy to pass through the thick, mustard-colored coat.

Roughly two minutes later, she curtsied in front of me. "I didn't check any inappropriate places, miss. But the only thing I saw was a big bruise on her right side."

Uh oh. The memory of meeting Gladys at the shack flashed through my mind with a clarity that had been missing before. Maybe my concussion was healing, returning the incident to my mind. Or maybe it was the bruise. Either way, I knew where the injury had come from. It would have been simpler if any evidence of my run-in with Gladys would've disappeared. Apparently, there were no secrets from the loop. Time to lay it all on the table. I owed my friend that much.

"I have a confession to make, guys. Earlier today, when I was walking the grounds, I had a confrontation with Gladys. That may have been what landed me in the wheelbarrow."

Beside the decedent, Sir Bogart stretched lazily

and fixed me with a smug grin. "Did you strike Mrs. Williams?"

I frowned as I began to explain what I recalled from the shack. I winced, waiting for dismay over my not telling them sooner. Yet it never came. Instead, they listened intently, asked a handful of questions, and finally seemed satisfied.

After multiple retellings of my crazy tale, the consensus was I hadn't killed Gladys Williams. In fact, Sir Bogart felt confident that she had been the culprit who dealt the blow to the back of my head and wheeled me to the gazebo.

"Oh. Wait right here." I ran to the front of the mansion, out the double doors, and around the exterior toward the gazebo.

The wheelbarrow was still there, but something seemed different now. Time to use everything I'd learned about tracking. It all came from books on Daniel Boone and other wilderness explorers, but I searched for tire tracks in the soft earth.

Hallelujah. There was a track leading to the back door of the manor. And some mud on the step. The mud seemed the same as any other mud on the property, so no clues there.

However, whoever had placed Gladys Williams's

body in the mudroom had clearly used the wheelbarrow to transport her. The unfortunate part of this clue was that someone had also transported me in that same wheelbarrow. Therefore, if I pointed out this particular piece of evidence to the sheriff, it would only serve to incriminate me further since my fingerprints and DNA would be mixed up with hers. There were many unhelpful ways that evidence could be construed.

Hurrying back into the manor, I shared my findings with the team. Norman shook his head. "That is perplexing, madam. But we have an advantage the sheriff does not possess."

Shrugging my shoulders, I stared at him in confusion. "And what would that be?"

He smiled politely. "We know, beyond a shadow of a doubt, that you did not kill Mrs. Williams."

My mouth twisted in a half-grin as their unwavering loyalty wasn't something I was used to. "Thank you. It means a lot to me that you guys believe in my innocence. I know she was alive when I left her. The thing is, I still don't understand what she's doing living in a shack on my property."

Sir Bogart nodded. "Perhaps the most judicious use of our time would be for someone to visit the Williams estate. We are unlikely to answer the question of her strange living arrangement without exploring that piece of the puzzle."

I put my hands on my hips and studied them. "Well, that sounds like a job for the human. I didn't ask before, but I'm assuming none of you can leave the manor. Is that correct?"

All three hastily nodded.

"I'll get my coat."

Silently, I slipped into it and hurried out the back door. Now that I thought about it, this was the path Gladys always seemed to take to and from the manor, so it must be the right way to reach her property, too.

Of course, I'd only ever seen Gladys disappear into the underbrush and wasn't exactly sure how to get to the Williams estate. So I headed to the stone pillar marking the corner of my property that Norman had mentioned butted up to hers, and I searched for any sign of a trail or path.

Eureka. There was an area that seemed too well traveled to be an accident.

Carefully following the faint trail through the tall pines eventually rewarded my efforts.

The once grand estate had fallen into horrific disrepair. Much like a book abandoned to the elements, the mansion seemed to disintegrate before my very eyes, and it caused a kind of sorrow I didn't expect. But I had answers to find.

I was under the impression Mrs. Williams lived alone, and the disrepair certainly implied she had no assistance, but I had no proof. It would be safest to approach with caution until I confirmed my suspicion.

Taking a few steps closer, I called, "Hello. Anybody there?" Then I stopped to listen for a response. Hearing none, I made my way toward the dilapidated home of the closest thing I had—or used to have—to an enemy.

Wow. The marble entry steps must've been something before the rust stains and deep cracks destroyed their fragile beauty.

Climbing the crumbling staircase, I kept my senses on high alert. Tacked onto the front door, for all to see, was a notice from the bank right beside another notice from the county.

The writing had faded with time. As near as I could tell, the property had been repossessed for unpaid property taxes over two years ago. Then, about six months ago, the entire property had been condemned.

There was a chance Gladys kept living here after the repossession. Squatters found abandoned places to live all the time, didn't they? It was a remote property, and the bank certainly wouldn't have had the manpower to check on it regularly.

The thought of her living in that ramshackle building on my property, with next to nothing, filled my heart with despair. Perhaps she'd only had to abandon the estate after it was condemned. Even with those parameters, it meant she'd been toughing it out all alone for over six months. What a terrible existence. Despite her behavior toward me, I would never wish such a life on her.

It would be best for me to return to Moonlight Manor and share my findings with the team, regroup, and make a plan. However, the little girl in me who read all of Charles Dickens' tales of woe wanted answers. That girl needed to explore.

Pushing on the front door, I gulped when it opened easily. It creaked on its rusty hinges, but didn't resist my touch. The papers nailed to the front flapped as a light breeze hit them.

When I entered the great hall, I instantly wished I hadn't. Sunlight streamed through multiple holes in the roof, and that wasn't even the worst of it. Vandals had carted off handles, chandeliers, and other high-end architectural pieces. Perhaps they were legitimate scrappers, with permission from the county, but a remote address like this one seemed a prime target for less than legal harvesting. And I doubted Gladys could have had the know-how or the strength of body to rob the place herself.

Six months in that shack . . . aging and alone . . . No matter how much I disliked her, my heart still ached for my neighbor. I couldn't bear to see anymore. Stepping out of the home, I closed the door and headed home in poor spirits.

When I trudged up the rear steps of my manor, I came in through the rear of the grand foyer and called out. "You guys are not going to believe— Sheriff Allen?" I stopped short. The sight of Haley in my foyer caught me off guard. Did one of the ghosts call her?

The sheriff's expression remained pinched. "Exactly when were you planning on calling this in, Miss Coleman?"

Glancing at the apparitions floating behind her, I searched for a guilty party. They all shook their heads. I turned to Haley. "Hmmmm? What are you talking about?"

"Well, Frannie Clark called the station and said you didn't sound like yourself. She asked me to make a health and welfare check. I rang the bell, but there was no answer, and I worried you could have been injured. All alone in this giant house . . . I let myself in and searched the property. Imagine my surprise when I found the corpse of Gladys Williams in your mudroom."

"Sheriff, I can explain."

Sheriff Allen shook her head, and the muscles in her jaw clenched. "So you knew about it? And you didn't make a report? Miss Coleman, I'm placing you under arrest on suspicion of—"

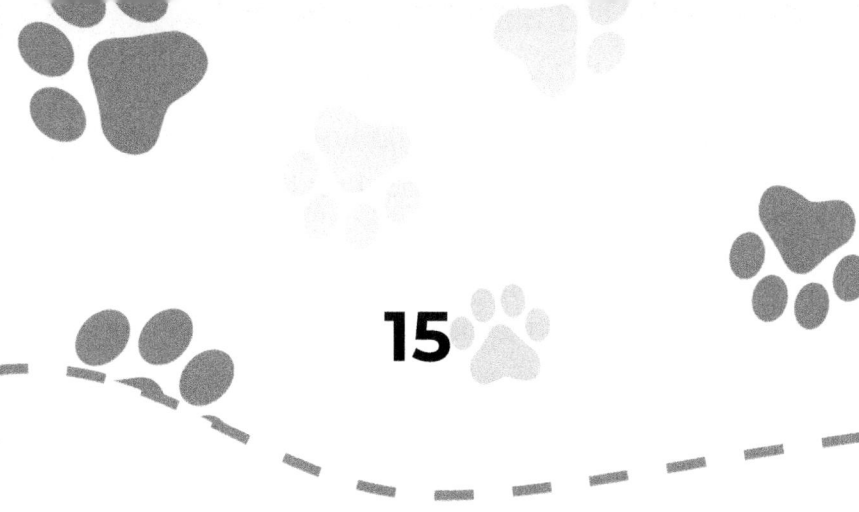

15

*"... All who dare to enter with ill intent,
Will relive their crime and death's punishment."*

A foul wind buffeted the attic and Sir Bogart's warning echoed from the rafters.

Great, here we go again.

Closing the grimoire and tucking it under my arm, I opened the trunk and grabbed the crystal ball. For half a second, I glared at the walls for sending me back here. If the grimoire poem had brought the house to life, it could handle a dark look or two. Figuring out how to get out of the time loop was necessary. We couldn't keep on like this.

No need to look within the orb's cloudy depths. I

already knew Frannie would arrive any minute. I hustled down the stairs, placed the book, and added the crystal ball to the display.

Next, I walked to the center of the grand entrance, directly below the three-tiered chandelier, and shouted, "Team meeting. Bogey. Norman. Velma. Front and center."

Moments later, the apparitions popped into being in front of me. Bogey took the lead without asking. Typical. "Before we proceed, I must inquire if everyone remembers?" All heads, ghostly and otherwise, nodded in agreement. "Very well. Then it is safe to assume that ours are the only actions that matter."

Shrugging, I gazed at the other members of the team. "Agreed. Do you think we should cancel the tours this time?"

Norman clasped his hands behind his back. "Perhaps, however, the visit from your redheaded friend, and her concern for your safety, is what triggered the arrival of the sheriff on our last go round. Until that unfortunate interruption, we were making progress."

There was no arguing with Norman's logic. Things had been going swimmingly until Frannie assumed I was crazy. "I could call her and tell her not to call the sheriff. That might work."

There were no cheers.

"Yeah, okay, that probably won't work. But canceling the tours doesn't seem to do the trick, either. Gladys still ended up dead, and I still wound up in handcuffs. What am I missing?"

Sir Bogart scoffed. "You have mentioned on more than one occasion, mistress, your need for funds. I say we keep our appointments with our guests for this evening and attempt to forestall the sheriff's arrival for as long as possible tomorrow. Do you remember the clues you gathered yesterday?"

Nodding, I went over the list and everyone agreed with the information I recalled.

Chewing my bottom lip, I considered what else there was. "What about my run in with Gladys out at the shack? Should I go back out there today?"

Norman shook his head fiercely. "I think not, madam. Nothing was gained, and in addition, that unfortunate kerfuffle resulted in a bruise on Mrs. Williams's side. Further implicating you in the violence against her person."

He had a point. "Good thinking, Norman. So, the tours are on, Frannie—"

A deep gonging from the doorbell resonated through the manor and I smiled half-heartedly. "Here goes nothing, guys. Let's hope we figure things out in the morning. In the meantime, I get to eat some delicious cupcakes, and tonight we get to party like it's 1999."

The ghosts all stared at me as though I'd finally cracked.

My shoulders drooped as I dropped the attempt at enthusiasm in the face of the drudgery of this crazy, grimoire-caused time loop. "It's a song about—never mind. I need to get the door."

On the other side of the threshold, Frannie smiled broadly and jiggled the pastry box back and forth. At least her enthusiasm was real. "Happy grand opening day."

I waved her through, leaning on the door knob like it was a life raft. "Come on in. I'll get the coffee brewing, and we can gossip over cupcakes. That's our thing, right?" I tried to mask the frustration in my voice.

Silently, she trailed after me into the kitchen. When I stopped at the coffee maker, she squinted, and her brown eyes held a mix of suspicion and hurt. "You seem kinda out of sorts? Did something go wrong with the prep?"

For an instant, I considered making something

up, but the words tumbled out of me before I could stop them. "Look, maybe it's because you don't actually live in the manor, but you're not retaining the memory of the loop as clearly as the rest of us. Trust me when I tell you, we've done this more times than I can count. So please ignore my exasperated attitude. If you'd lived through the next twenty-four hours as many times as I have, you'd be at the end of your rope, too."

She dropped onto a chair in the corner of the kitchen and her eyes suddenly widened with shock. "Is Gladys Williams dead?"

My hand, complete with a measured scoop of coffee grounds, froze in midair. Turning toward Frannie with extreme caution, I hoped I'd heard her correctly. "So you do remember?"

Frannie scraped her curly red hair back from her face and rubbed her temples. "I thought it was all a weird dream. But this does seem sorta familiar. What's going on, Syd?"

Struggling to swallow, I took a deep breath. My hand shook, scattering coffee grounds on the floor. "If I tell you, will you promise not to call Sheriff Allen and ask her to do a health and welfare check on me?"

Her mouth hung open for a second. "Did I do that?"

"You did. Or you do, tomorrow. The problem is, this time loop thingy resets every time Sheriff Allen gets here and arrests me for the murder. The handcuffs click, and I'm stuck in the same day again. So, whatever you do, please do not call her. Promise me, Frannie."

"I promise. I'll write myself a note—"

"Don't bother. Every time the loop resets, anything we do differently disappears. It's the most frustrating thing that's ever happened to me. We were so close to figuring it out this morning." Frustrating was the kindest term for whatever this was, and I couldn't imagine going through this one more time. I returned to my coffee-making task to keep from bursting into tears.

"But Gladys Williams is alive. She came in—"

"I know. She came in and bought a dozen donuts." A thrill of newness sparks through my heart. "Hold on. How did she pay for those donuts?"

Frannie's eyebrows pinched, and she shook her head. "Oh, she didn't pay for them. She takes them over to the volunteers at the animal shelter. I just give them to her. You know, pay it forward and all that."

Pressing brew on the coffeemaker, I paced around the butcher-block island, talking more to myself than anyone else. "So Frannie gives her free doughnuts.

She's living in a rent-free shack on my property, and she probably steals the canned goods from Hannaford's and hides them under that hideous coat. You gotta admire the old girl's tenacity."

Frannie rose from her chair and intercepted me with a gentle arm around my shoulders. "I know I promised not to call Sheriff Allen, but you're sounding a little crazy. Why on earth would Gladys be living on your property? She has her own… Doesn't she?"

A sigh deflated me. "I have no idea, Frannie. And trust me, I'd take you out there and show you right now, but I can't afford to leave a bruise on Gladys that could link back to me or have my DNA end up in the wheelbarrow."

My wonderful, trusting friend pulled me to a chair at the table and forced me to sit. "Okay, you're freaking me out, Sydney. What are you talking about?" She knelt beside me with one hand, gently patting my knee. "Explain it all."

After taking a deep breath, I attempted to share the details of the most recent loop, and my discoveries at the Williams estate.

Frannie stood and covered her mouth with her hand. Eventually, she let out a long, low whistle and returned to her chair at the table. "Unbelievable. So she's been living alone in a shack for maybe the last two years?"

"For sure, the last six months at least." The sorrow over Gladys Williams's situation echoed in my voice. The coffee maker beeped. I moved to get out of my chair, but Frannie waved me back.

"I've got the coffee. Sit tight." She grabbed some plates and cutlery, then brought the coffees to the table. I powered through two caramel-apple cupcakes while I listened to her theorize about the upcoming murder.

"So you had a run-in with her. Augusta Adams threatened her right in front of you, and she had a heated argument with Rodney. Although, technically, you're the one that threatened her at the end of that argument."

Since my mouth was full, all I could do was shrug and nod.

"Well, I have to agree with what you told me Norman said. We all know you didn't kill Gladys. So that leaves two suspects. Augusta and Rodney. Didn't you say Augusta came on one of the tours?"

I washed the last bite of cupcake down with a slug of coffee. "That's right. She'll be in the third tour group tonight. At least since we haven't canceled any of the tours this time through."

Frannie clapped, and I winced at the sound. "There you have it," she said. "She used the tour group as her way in, and then she killed Gladys."

My gaze narrowed as I tried to process the memory fragments. "It's not super clear, but I could swear I checked the mudroom after the third tour on one of the loops."

Frannie nodded and strummed her fingers on the ancient oak. "Sure, but it would take some time to walk over to the estate in the dark, kill someone, and bring them back here."

Shaking my head, I tapped my finger on the table beside hers. "You're forgetting, Gladys wasn't at the estate. She was in the shack."

"You don't know that, Sydney. Maybe she's the one taking things from her old home. In fact, she may be the one that sold off the chandelier, and all the other stuff you mentioned. Or at least maybe hired someone to do that."

My girl had a decent point. I had absolutely no idea where Gladys was the night of her murder. And I also hadn't made a thorough check of the wheelbarrow tracks. Sure, there was a track leading back to where it had been parked, but I'd foolishly forgotten to see where else it might lead—like to the Williams estate in particular. Hmm. Maybe I wasn't as great an investigator as I thought I was.

"Tomorrow morning, the first thing I'll check is if there are any tracks leading to the hidden path. If Gladys was killed at her old mansion, and someone wheeled her all the way over. There'll be a deep rut. Which I would've totally obscured when I went tramping over there. Or wait, was that before she was killed? Oh man, this looping is messing with my head. I can't keep anything straight."

Frannie leaned toward me. "What about the ghosts? If they're remembering, are they getting confused like you?"

"No, they seemed pretty sure about everything. Maybe I'll go over all the details that I remember with them, and they can keep me from making mistakes tomorrow."

She nodded and smiled brightly. "Perfect. Everyone doing what they do best. If we all work together, I know we can figure this out. Everyone in town may have had run-ins with Gladys Williams, but I think we've actually narrowed it down to the two most likely suspects."

"Fiddlesticks." Smacking my forehead with the heel of my hand, I shook my head. "Nope. On one loop, I invited Rodney to come back out that evening and take a tour, but he said he couldn't make it because he had to take his kids costume shopping."

Frannie inhaled sharply. "Rodney got divorced after that big scandal—the one he and Gladys were arguing about. His wife took the kids and moved to Indiana."

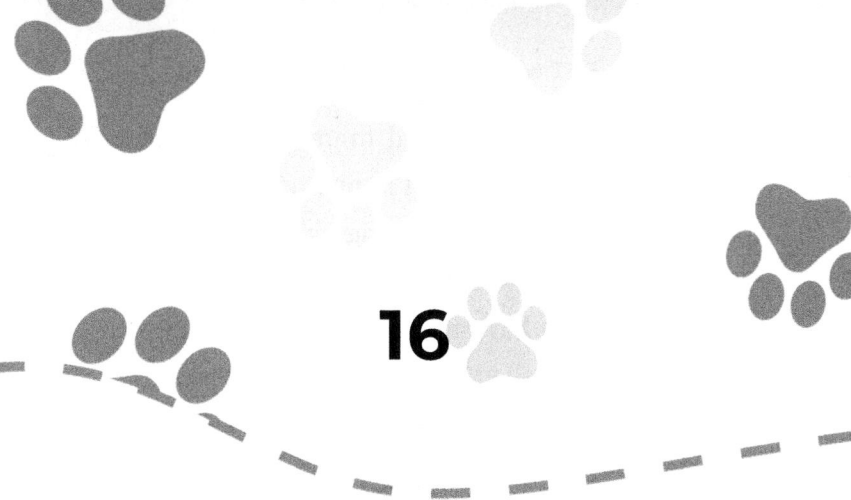

16

An eerie silence hung in the air, while Frannie and I stared across the table at one another. Indiana? His wife moved to Indiana with the kids?

I was the first to find my voice and utter what we were both thinking. "If Rodney lied, then—"

Frannie waved her hands and reached across the table. "Let's not jump to conclusions. Maybe his children are visiting. I mean, he probably has visitation. Right?"

Taking a moment to swallow and sort out my thoughts, I attempted to answer. "Sure. He might have visitation. It seems like an odd time of year, though. Don't you think? Thanksgiving break would be next month, and winter break in December.

Unless things have changed dramatically since you and I went to school, I don't remember a long enough break in October to justify flying kids from Indiana to Maine. Not even with the fall break some schools have. I think we have to look at the very real possibility that Rodney lied."

She nodded, took a sip of coffee, and strummed her fingers on the table. "Okay. True. Maybe it was an innocent lie, though. Maybe he really hates the idea of haunted mansion tours and lied to spare your feelings. That's a thing, isn't it?"

Lying to spare someone's feelings was absolutely, definitely a thing. I'd done it plenty of times myself. "Sure, Frannie. Though, I'm still not convinced. Rodney doesn't strike me as that kind of guy. It's not like he held anything back in that spat with Gladys. Honestly, hurting her feelings seemed like the least of his worries."

She nodded. "Yes, but he has a history with Gladys. If what he said was even half true, the trouble she caused was part of the reason he lost his business and his family. The difference is, there's no bad blood between you and him. You know what I mean? So it's entirely possible that he would lie to spare your feelings. It's not far-fetched. Really, I don't think it is."

There was definitely a ring of truth to Frannie's theory. In fact, I had basically defended Rodney against Gladys. "I can see where you're coming from. It's entirely possible that Rodney lied to spare my feelings. However, I don't think we can take him off the suspect list."

Frannie poured a little hotter-upper of coffee into my mug. "I agree. I better get back to the bakery."

I grazed Frannie's elbow as she moved away to return the pot to the maker. "Thanks for making the trip out, Frannie. And I'm not just saying that because of the cupcakes. I genuinely enjoy the company."

She chuckled and headed toward the front doors. "Me too."

Walking her out, I stopped at the bottom step and gripped her shoulder. "Whatever you do tomorrow, do not call Sheriff Allen. Understood?"

She grinned. "So you're telling me you *are* crazy, but I should completely ignore it and leave you to your possible horrible demise?"

I gave her a playful shove toward her vehicle. "Not funny. Solving this mystery hinges on me getting as much time as I possibly can to chase down these clues. If you call the sheriff, it will toss a giant wrench into everything."

"I promise I'll do my best, Sydney. And I really hope you and the ghosts figure it all out. I wish there was something we could do to prevent the death of Gladys, but I suppose you already tried that."

"In a sense. We thought if we canceled all the tours and changed some other things, that would prevent the suspect from gaining access to the house. But now that I've discovered the additional clues, I'm almost certain that Gladys wasn't killed in the house. It's no coincidence that the wheelbarrow suddenly entered the loop. It has to play an important role."

Frannie opened the door of her vehicle, and I gave one last wave. "I hope to see you tomorrow—and the next day. And by tomorrow I mean, I hope tomorrow doesn't end up being today." She wagged her head from side to side and circled her finger at her temple.

As she drove away, I sat down on the granite steps, tucked my chin in my palm, placed my elbow on my knee, and stared up at Aphrodite. "Am I losing my mind, beautiful goddess? I know your thing is love and not murder loops, but I could use some help."

I studied the time-worn face of the goddess Aphrodite, half expecting her lips to move, but I experienced no such luck. Even with ghosts, a grimoire, and a magical crystal ball in my life, I had trouble getting outside help on our mystery.

I dropped my hand. That settles it. I've lost my mind, and even the statues have given up on me. Though, I hadn't checked with the gargoyles on the roof, had I? I mentally scoffed at myself. Climbing to my feet, I stretched. Time to get this show on the road.

Today, I couldn't be bothered by checklists. If it was done, great. If it wasn't, I no longer cared. Since I'd tried everything I could think of at Moonlight Manor, I threw on a coat and wandered over to the Williams estate without letting the ghosts know where I'd gone.

It was currently about the time of day I ran into Gladys at the shack on the previous loop. So I now felt mostly confident that no one would be at her condemned mansion.

Nevertheless, I hung to the trees and circled around to the back, carefully listening and watching for tell-tale signs of anybody there. There were three entrances at the rear of the home. Large double doors led into the main hall, and single doors on either wing which led somewhere. I'd have to get closer to see where those went.

I tiptoed along the overgrown hedge and up the

cracked stone steps at the rear. The handle was missing on the single door on the left side, and I used the edge of my shirt to grip the wood and pull it open. Last time, I pushed against the front door without thinking and probably left fingerprints. I would not make that amateur mistake again.

This wing of the home hadn't seen as much damage as the front entrance. The roof was still intact, and the textiles were fairing much better. The windows had a northern exposure, so no direct sunlight was fading the fabrics. There were lovely drapes, an enormous tapestry, and a decent rug on the floor.

Odd. Maybe textiles didn't fetch the same price as hardware. But the pieces seemed in good shape. Perhaps more care had been given to this end of the estate.

I quietly approached the door of the study and peeked around the corner. My breath caught in my throat as I heard shuffling footsteps and the tap of a walking stick. My throat dried, my stomach twisted, and my skin prickled.

Shoot. Gladys must've been here before she went to the shack. The last thing I needed was for her to catch me snooping around her house. All the things she said about me would certainly be true. I had to get out of here.

Easing back to the thick carpeting, I tiptoed toward the open back door. However, when I reached it, I saw Gladys stepping unsteadily down the stairs leading out of the double doors. I ducked down below the window and counted to fifty. It was a trick I'd always used with my brothers. They loved to play hide and seek, and they also loved to play tricks on me. Their favorite one was pretending they found everyone when I was the last one left. The winner.

There were several times when I had popped out of my hiding place, only to discover that one of my weaselly brothers had lied, and I'd lost my win. Eventually, I learned to sit quietly in my excellent hiding space and count to fifty. My rambunctious brothers were all enormously impatient, and my counting usually worked. Soon, I actually started to win. Of course, they immediately changed the game because no one likes their little sister to win.

When I reached fifty, I carefully peeked over the ledge of the window into the backyard. No sign of the stick-shaking woman or her mustard yellow coat. It was deserted. Now that the place was empty, I could take a look around, but the fear that went along with almost getting caught a few minutes ago hadn't subsided. I took a step, and the sound echoed through the mansion, sending my heart racing once more. Making a decision was necessary since I couldn't stand here in indecision, but after the close call, I didn't think I could explore.

Instead, I made my way back outside, keeping an eye out for my down-on-her-luck neighbor as I returned to the trail at a leisurely pace. If I'd gotten my timing right, she should be headed back to the shack.

When I reached Moonlight Manor, I had an idea, an epiphany almost. A pretty good one, if I said so myself. I hopped in Blue Bell and drove to the sheriff's station. The red brick exterior was the warmest thing about the structure. The interior was spartan, cold, and wholly utilitarian.

I slammed the driver's door on Blue Bell and marched inside, determined to face this head on.

Sheriff Allen was at her scarred wooden desk. Her Smokey Bear style hat sat atop an old file cabinet on her left. She looked up as soon as I darkened her doorway and gestured to the cushioned seat on the other side of her desk. "Hey, Sydney. What brings you in?"

The offered seat squeaked as I settled in it. "I'm sure you knew this, but it came as a surprise to me. I wasn't aware that the old Williams estate was abandoned. And condemned."

The sheriff nodded her head solemnly. "Yeah, real shame. After her husband passed away, she couldn't afford the upkeep. She was never good with money, but when Maynard was alive, he kept her spending in line and paid all the bills on time. Once he was gone, things kind of spiraled."

"Has someone filed a permit to salvage items from the property?" I leaned closer, hoping Haley would pick up on the importance of investigating things for Gladys.

Sheriff Allen sat up straight and tilted her head to the side. "Not to my knowledge. I would definitely have been informed. Why do you ask?"

"I went for a walk this morning. That's how I discovered the place had been abandoned. A lot of hardware and other valuable architectural pieces are missing. If it wasn't a legal salvage job, then it's probably the work of vandals." I nearly cringed since I'd placed myself in the list of suspects again by admitting, should they find Gladys Williams dead, but I didn't care. Handcuffs reset the timeline, and I needed to solve the mystery of her death.

She sighed and shook her head. "It's possible. But part of me is pretty sure that Gladys is selling off her own stuff. If the bank is willing to look the other way, I'm not one to hassle an old lady for trying to put food on her table."

"I hear what you're saying. It's a real shame. Looks like it was a pretty beautiful home at one time."

"Absolutely. Is there anything else?"

"Not today." Part of me wanted to warn her about the imminent doom that would befall Gladys Williams, but, thankfully, a bigger part of me realized that would only make me look doubly guilty later.

Avoiding the cuffs would be hard enough in this version of the loop.

17

Safely back at Moonlight Manor, it was time for me to get trussed up like a Christmas goose. However, I had learned my lesson about historic ensembles and my inability to complete them on my own. So I made my way to my room and laid the dress on my bed.

"Velma?" I called to the empty space. "Oh, Velma, dear. I would love some help with my wardrobe for the tours."

The eager-to-please ghost drifted into the blue room and curtsied. "Happy to help, miss."

Layer upon layer, we proceeded. Hooks, straps, buttons, and buckles. Heaven only knew how much time later, I was finally dressed. I adjusted my bonnet and even pulled a few strands of hair loose, allowing them to curl around my face.

"How do I look?"

"Like the proper mistress of Moonlight Manor." Velma beamed at me." I'll take your cloak and gloves downstairs, miss."

Velma floated off with the rest of my garments, and I stared at myself in the cerulean-trimmed mirror. Gone was the sleek, polished, über professional woman. But along with that façade, the tiny stress lines around my eyes and the never-ending tightness in my shoulders had also disappeared.

Despite the ups and downs of this looping roller coaster, I somehow still felt more relaxed than I'd ever been in New York. Which was something considering I had three ghosts and a fresh corpse recurring on loop.

Misty Meadows was more than just some random town where I'd ended up. Misty Meadows was quickly becoming my home. People like Frannie and Davis, and even *lobstah* Craig, were friends. Friends I could count on and people who actually showed up when I called them.

On the day Lucas Aconite dumped me, and I had tucked my tail between my legs to run away from everything I thought I wanted, I never would've admitted the truth. And even with all the current problems I faced with murder accusations and time loops and struggling business ventures, I still wouldn't trade my haunted new life for the world.

Taking a deep breath, I smiled at myself in the mirror. "You did not kill Gladys Williams. And this time, you're going to prove it."

If the creepy spell I'd recited from the Blodfyss sisters' grimoire had actually brought this house to life, as I suspected, I hoped declaring my innocence to it would affect the outcome in a positive way. Besides manifesting wouldn't hurt anything.

I lifted my skirts, marched downstairs and out onto the front terrace to await the arrival of the first tour group.

Once again, everything went exactly as it had gone innumerable times before, but as Frannie left, I gripped her arm and whispered one last time. "Remember, do not call Sheriff Allen."

She gave me a thumbs up and nodded sharply. "You got it."

The second group had always been a bit of a conundrum. At least ten of the fifteen members were children, who appeared to be under the age of nine. Not that I was good at guessing the ages of children, but they were rambunctious, immature, and had no verbal filter. Exactly as I remembered my brothers growing up together on the farm.

I kept my general announcements more playful, and Sir Bogart made several appearances to the elation of the youngsters. He twitched his tail, cleaned his whiskers, and pounced on imaginary, invisible mice. When I pretended he caught the last one, all the kids cheered as Sir Bogart trotted into another room.

When we moved into the ballroom, Velma began to play *Camptown Races*. Most of the children were familiar with the tune, even if they didn't know the words. They couldn't see Velma, only hear the piano. I didn't know all the words, but I sang the chorus aloud and some parents joined in. The children began an impromptu dance around the magnificent ballroom, and it warmed my heart.

Frannie had mentioned something about Scrooge-themed haunted tours for Christmas. Maybe what I needed to do was throw an exclusive ticketed gala. I'd have her help me create an outstanding menu, a live string quartet, black tie, of course—

"Miss? Miss, can we see more?" A little girl with red pigtails was tugging on my cloak.

I grinned down at her. "Of course, dear. Follow me and let's see if we can find that naughty kitty."

When we headed up the imperial staircase, Sir Bogart bounded down the right-hand flight, across the landing, and up the left-hand flight. The children squealed with delight.

Rather than drag the group through each of the bedrooms, reciting boring bits of architectural information, I changed it up. "Let's see if we can catch that kitty."

The children all cheered and raced up the steps.

The parents and I made a slower ascent. One of the frazzled-looking mothers sighed with relief. "Thanks for that. Those kids have ten times as much energy as me, and sometimes I really need a break."

I laughed but couldn't actually relate. Back when things had been super intense with Lucas, the idea of children had popped into my head once or twice, but quickly exited. I'd only seen one pregnant woman around the Aconite Agency, and she never returned from maternity leave. Now that I'd relocated to a quiet country manor, maybe it was time to reconsider my future. I could only imagine how much children would enjoy growing up with Sir Bogart around, and he had been quite fond of Haley—Sheriff Allen—when she was a child, visiting the abandoned manor.

A loud crash from somewhere near the lavender

room snapped me from my reverie. "Oh dear, I hope no one was hurt."

The lackadaisical parents suddenly found loads of their own energy as we all raced toward the recent sound.

A large suit of armor had fallen over—or been tipped. Fortunately, it missed the fingers, toes, and limbs of all children present. The wild gaggle took turns accusing each other, and the parents all apologized profusely.

Despite the mess and work they caused, I beamed at them, relieved nobody had gotten hurt. "I wouldn't worry about it, folks. Any knight worth his salt should be able to survive an attack from an army of children."

The laughter was quick through the crowd, but nervous.

Spreading my arms to take in the fallen armor. "Honestly, don't worry about a thing. Besides, who knows if the kids were even to blame? With all the spooky things happening in the mansion, maybe a ghost knocked over the knight."

Eager to see the blame placed elsewhere, the children jumped up and down and cheered in agreement. With no injuries, there'd be no claims on my insurance, and I could keep moving forward on my intentions for Moonlight Manor. Though, maybe I needed to have a chat with Sir Bogart about letting the younger visitors chase him too close to armor.

I gestured toward the hallway. "Now, if you'll all follow me to the last stop on the tour, we might have one last chance to catch that feisty feline. We're headed to that large room at the front of the house, by the round tower, with a bright-red door knob."

The children raced ahead, and once they were out of earshot, I shared the spooky story of Beatrix de Haviland's murder with only the adults.

One of the mothers gripped my arm. "Thank you so much for not saying that in front of the children. My little Cheyenne has enough trouble sleeping."

Murmurs of agreement passed through the crowd, and when we entered the burgundy room, the children were all gathered around the glowing specter of Sir Bogart posing magnificently on the red and gold duvet.

I laughed. "Oh my goodness, children. You must all be especially good boys and girls. Sir Bogart rarely makes an appearance in this room."

The children clapped their hands, and some reached out to pet the kitty. Sir Bogart made a show of flickering and then popping out of sight.

The kids gasped with excitement.

"I have one more surprise for you." I opened the secret passage, but, when the door creaked backward, I was the one who received a surprise. Velma popped out, and I nearly tripped over a tiny girl with dark-brown braids when I jumped.

"Beggin' your pardon, miss. I only thought it would be fun for the little ones to follow me down the passage."

I pressed a hand to my heart and glanced at the group. They were beyond enthralled. Though, the children had all backed away and gripped onto their respective parents. Even the parents' eyes widened.

I turned to the captive audience. "You'll have to excuse me, boys and girls. I'm still getting used to the surprises this house holds for me. Lucky for you, Velma is a friendly ghost. She said she'd be happy to lead you all to safety down in the drawing room. Just follow her through the secret passage, and I'll join you in a moment."

Velma beckoned them with her hand, and the precocious girl with the red pigtails was the first to step forward.

Once the ice had been broken, the rest of the group fell in line, and Velma led them down the twisting tunnel. I followed at a leisurely pace, letting them all enjoy being so close to an apparition.

Finally, I gave my closing speech in the drawing room and promised plenty of exciting sweet treats at the Halloween feast. Each of the parents thanked me as they left, and several of the children waved.

Luckily, I stopped myself from mentioning the blood red liquid pouring from Aphrodite's vase. Although, when I looked at the water, it actually had a golden, sparkling hue. It was almost as if—

When I gazed into the moonlit face of the goddess of love, I could have sworn her stone eyelid winked in my direction. Would the wonders of Moonlight Manor never cease?

There were no anomalies to report on tours three or four. And nobody in the mudroom after either. Perhaps we'd earned a break from impending doom. I dared not hope, but I would take the lull anyway.

After spending hours in the period shoes, my feet hurt like the dickens, and I wanted nothing more than my glorious mug of tea, and a few hours' sleep. Velma would be waking me up soon enough. Yet as I drifted off, I couldn't shake my optimism about this time through.

Morning found me snug in my bed as Velma slipped quietly into my room. The blue drapes fluttered as she opened them. "Good morning, miss. I wanted to let you know that there is a corpse in the mudroom. But I remembered, miss. And I didn't do no screamin' today. I thought I'd let you have a bit of a lie in."

I hid a yawn behind my hand, feeling more rested than I had in . . . well, I didn't know how long I'd been in this loop. "Thank you, Velma. That was very thoughtful. I'll be down in a few minutes, so we can get started on the investigation. Let's all cross our fingers that we find the end of this today."

She curtsied, and, as she vanished through the wall, called from the ether, "From your mouth to God's ear, miss."

18

When I wandered into the kitchen in jeans, a sweater, and my hair swirled into a messy bun, Velma already had coffee brewing in the pot and eggs frying on the stove.

My sniff was long and appreciative. "That smells wonderful. I'm a lot hungrier than I thought I was."

Velma smiled as she poured the coffee and plated my breakfast. "That's good to hear, miss. You need some meat on them bones."

Laughing so hard I almost choked, I tried to explain the twenty-first century beauty standards to my lovely, curvy apparition. The eggs sizzled in the skillet.

She scowled at me with a motionless spatula in her hand and a hint of horror in her expression.

Finally, she blinked. "That ain't right, miss. It's not healthy to be so fragile as to be blown over by a stiff breeze."

I chuckled, shook my head, and took a seat at my table.

"Oh, your eggs be ready, miss," she said, spinning back to the stove. "Nearly let those get away from me." She put the eggs on a plate and carefully placed them on the table before me. "It's simpler than most meals here back when I were alive, but here's a nice dollop of butter." She pointed to the yellow tab on the edge of the plate. Then she took the dishes to the sink.

Shoving a delicious bite of fried egg into my mouth, I nodded in agreement. "I'm learning, Velma. You keep feeding me like this, and I'll be able to withstand a hurricane."

Chuckling, she scrubbed the frying pan. "What will you be up to today, miss?"

Another bite later, I answered. "I'm going to take everything I learned from my years of reading about other people's adventures and build a case."

She dried the pan and floated upward to hang it back on its hook. "Against who? Have you solved it, miss?"

"Not yet. But I'm hoping it's going to be one of

those 'build it and they will come' scenarios." I stared thoughtfully out the window and drummed my fingers on the table. "I'll gather every bit of evidence I can, and then, if we're lucky, the true guilty party will emerge. Perhaps we already have all the information we need, and simply need to put it together in the right way."

Wiping her hands on her apron, she smiled encouragingly. "That sounds right smart, miss."

Since Gladys was already dead, and I was mostly confident that Sheriff Allen wasn't going to show up, I could take my time and do some actual, honest-to-goodness sleuthing for clues without threat of being caught.

The sky outside was gray and hung low with worrisome clouds. The tops of the trees bending against the force of the wind, so I bundled up before heading out to see what I could see.

Once outside, I chose my steps carefully. The last thing I wanted to do was step on any evidence. I needed to figure out as much as I could about the wheelbarrow.

Behind my home, there were several different footprints. But that was to be expected with Augusta, her crew, Davis, and Rodney, all working on different projects inside and around the mansion.

Then I examined the tire track leading from the back door to where the wheelbarrow was currently parked. It wasn't a clear, single track, and the wild dying grass definitely obscured the detail. However, it wasn't terribly deep. I stepped over that mark and searched for a track heading in the other direction.

If there was something—

There it was. A deep rut in the damp earth. And this was a clear single track. I walked carefully several feet to the side of the track. There appeared to be some footprints as well, but my expertise didn't extend to discerning the differences between them. The tire track definitely came from Gladys Williams's property. Which meant that Gladys had been placed in the wheelbarrow and brought here, didn't it? Perhaps the wheelbarrow belonged to Gladys.

When I reached the path between the properties, I almost stepped on a second track, which showed that the wheelbarrow had been brought over to her property by a different route. *Interesting.*

My progress to the dilapidated Williams estate was slow, since I had to make my way through the tall grass and dead weeds beside the path. I didn't want to risk destroying any evidence.

As I reached the clearing around the Williams's

manor, I could easily see how the track ran straight through the untrimmed lawn and stopped in the dirt.

Odd. It was as though the wheelbarrow had been parked and then—

Was that a tire print from a vehicle?

It may not have rained for a few days, but the heavy morning dew and whatever other moisture hung in the air kept the soil damp enough to receive an imprint of a large tire tread. Maybe a truck or an SUV? I couldn't be sure. The tread wasn't extremely clean, but it was something.

A rumble of thunder and a glance toward the sky told me it may not be there for much longer, and I needed to preserve the evidence. I hurried back to my mansion as quickly as I could without stepping on the actual trail.

"Norman? Velma? Do you have any plaster of Paris?"

The ghosts shook their heads but Norman rubbed an ethereal hand along his chin. "What is its purpose, madam?"

"I need to make a cast of a tire print I found outside Gladys's old place." I resisted the urge to tap my foot on the floor. If I didn't make it back to the Williams's manor quickly, I'd lose the print entirely.

He lifted a finger and smiled knowingly. "Wait

right here, madam. I may have a solution." He disappeared and returned several minutes later with a weathered cardboard box and a smile.

The wind outside picked up, and the sky darkened. The treetops whipped back and forth more violently than before. Velma floated nearby, anxious but remaining quiet as Norman helped me.

He handed the carton to me.

I frowned at the contents. "What do I do with this?"

The ghostly butler waved toward the cardboard container. "If you mix this calcium hydroxide with sand and water, you can create a lime plaster, madam."

As he attempted to explain the ratios to me, my sleep-deprived brain finally clicked. "Oh, me."

Norman stopped speaking. "What is it, miss?"

"I don't know how I didn't think of it sooner, Norman. How stupid of me." Removing my cell phone from my jacket, I waved it. "Pictures are instant. No worrying about the rain washing evidence away. This is the difference between reading things in books and doing them in real life. I'll be back in a flash."

Norman nodded politely, but he seemed disappointed by my modern shortcut.

With my new photographic evidence idea at the forefront, I took pictures of the wheelbarrow, the tracks at the back door, the mud on the step, and even a short video of the tracks leading from Gladys Williams's place.

Next, I hurried through the long weeds beside the trail, and took more pictures of the vehicle track in the dirt.

A light sprinkle of rain dampened the top of my head, so I ducked and hurried home. When I reached the warmth of my rain-free foyer, I'd already thought of another lead.

I scrolled through my recent calls and selected a number. It rang once. "Davis, it's Sydney. Yes, the Sydney from Moonlight Manor." He really was too sweet for his own good. "I was wondering if you knew where I might find authentic hardware and lighting to do some renovations at the manor."

I put the phone on speaker so I could get out of my jacket and light the fire Norman had prepared in the drawing room. It took three attempts to start the blaze.

"Is it totally above board, Miss Sydney?" He sounded a bit hesitant to ask.

"Sydney. Just Sydney. And I'm not sure I know what you mean."

He inhaled sharply and blew a raspberry through his lips. "Well, you didn't hear from me, but there are legal dealers, and less-than-legal dealers. I know price is an issue, Sydney. So that's why I asked."

That confirmed my suspicion. Absolutely everyone in town knew my business. Though, it shouldn't surprise me. "If pricing were an issue, who would you suggest I call?"

He hesitated, but eventually answered. "I know you're a capable woman, Sydney. But I'd prefer if you'd let me make the call. Tell me what you're looking for, and I'll get you a good price."

What a sweetheart. It almost sounded like he was willing to break the law for me. Maybe I'd sworn off men a moment too soon. "I know this is a big ask in such a small town, but can you keep a secret, Davis?"

"Seems like it." He offered no further assurances.

"I think someone is illegally salvaging items from the Williams estate. I was hoping to find out who had those items for sale, and maybe trace it back to the person who'd been stealing from the property."

He blew out a long breath. "Boy, that does not sound good. Are you sure it wasn't Gladys? I'd heard she'd fallen on hard times."

"It could be. Let me see if I can come up with a good item for you to track down, and then we'll know for sure where the dealer got it. If it was from a crabby old lady in an ugly yellow coat—or somebody else."

Davis laughed. "You're not a fan of Mrs. Williams, are you?"

"Not exactly. Give me a few minutes. And I'll call you back."

Norman floated into the drawing room. "I didn't intend to eavesdrop, madam. But I may be able to help you in identifying items missing from next-door. Back when I was alive, I courted a lady's maid from the estate. Of course, after Mistress de Haviland's death, the woman abandoned me without explanation. I'm sure it was difficult for her to imagine being involved with a cat's valet."

Warming my hands by the fire, I nodded. "I'm sure you're right. Although, we are all servants of the cat at this point, aren't we?"

When Norman chuckled, I could see the handsome man he must have been in life. "Tell me what you know, miss, and I will do my level-best to help."

I thought a moment, rubbing my hands together in the heat from the fire. "Well, when I peeked in the front door, I noticed there was no chandelier in the grand entrance. Do you remember any details about that piece?"

He clasped his hands behind him and nodded. "I do. It was a particular point of pride for their family. I believe it had been imported from France and was hung with genuine quartz crystal drops. I regret I can't recall the story of the fixture's origin, but I'm sure Augusta Adams could fill in the details."

"So you heard her spouting off on the tour as well?"

He smiled and nodded, but he made no audible reply.

"That one item, as unique as it was, should be enough to get Davis on the right track. Thanks, Norman."

He bowed and drifted out of the room. I tapped redial on my phone and continued to warm myself by the fire.

"That was fast, Sydney. What did you find?"

I hadn't thought of how I would explain getting the information. Then I remembered good old cameras. "I found some old photos. There was a gorgeous chandelier that used to hang in the grand entrance. The drops were authentic quartz crystal. Do you think that's enough to go on?"

There was a brief pause. "How many tiers?"

Shoot. This is why lying was so much work. "Hold on a minute. I need to go check the photo." I tapped mute and ran to the foyer. "Norman. Norman, I have another question."

He popped in right in front of my face, and I had to admit a little scream escaped.

"I'm terribly sorry, madam."

"It's fine. How many tiers was the chandelier?"

"Five, madam."

"Perfect." I turned back toward the drawing room, paused, and called over my shoulder. "You better join me, in case there are any other questions."

Norman swooped in beside me as I unmuted the call. "Okay, it's five tiers," I said.

There was another pause on the other end of the line, and I imagined Davis was making notes. "Got it. And was it electric, gas, or did it still have candles?"

I gazed pleadingly at Norman.

"Originally gas, converted to electric madam." I repeated the information for Davis, and Norman and I managed to answer a couple of additional questions.

"I'll look into this, Sydney. If I find someone who's got this piece, what do you want me to do?"

"Tell them you represent a moneyed buyer from New York. And then see if you can get some information about where it came from or who sold it to them. Maybe make up some kind of story about the buyer wanting to know the history of the piece. I don't know. But it would be great if we could find out if Gladys was selling the pieces on her own, or if someone was stealing from her old property."

"You got it, boss." Davis ended the call, and I glanced toward Norman and chuckled.

"I suppose when you're the size of that guy," I said, "you don't worry about dealing with shady characters, but this whole cloak and dagger thing gives me the chills."

Norman nodded. "I'm not even alive, madam, and I'm frightened."

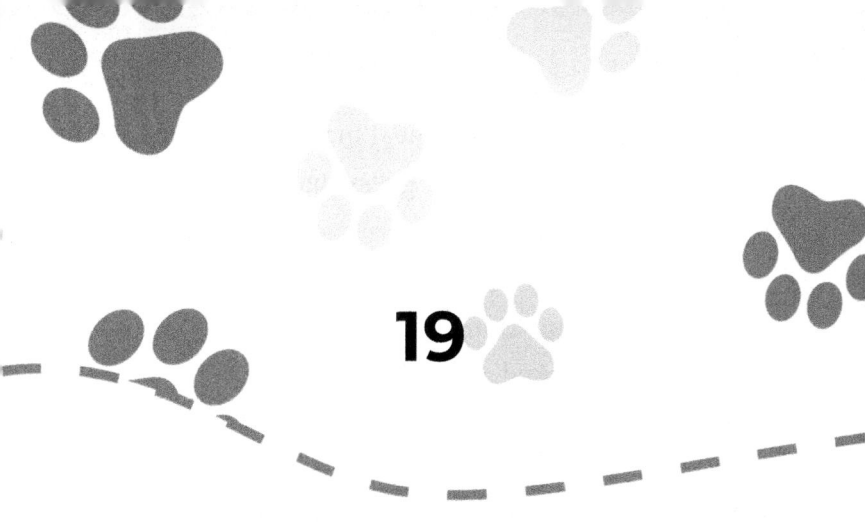

19

Recent events were taking their toll on my mind and body, and I nodded off without meaning to. When the ringing of my phone roused me from my accidental snooze in the drawing room, I grabbed it without thinking.

I didn't recognize the voice speaking on the other end. "Who is this?"

It was Rodney Finley calling to collect his final payment. But what struck me as odd was how he specifically asked if I'd looked at the door and if I needed him to make any changes.

Definitely weird.

And maybe even a bit suspicious too. Maybe a lot suspicious considering what I'd been looking into regarding Gladys's murder.

"No. Everything looks fine. I'm happy to make the final payment . . . Today? I guess that will work, but you'll have to hurry. I have to get ready for the tours tonight."

The timeframe didn't seem to concern him. But he sounded surprised about the tours.

"I'll see you in a little while," he said and ended the call.

Fiddlesticks. Why did I say yes without giving myself more time to think? Did I just invite a murderer to my house? As I lowered the phone, I couldn't stop my thoughts from tumbling end over end.

Before I had a chance to plan my next move, the phone rang again. "Frannie, I'm so glad you called."

She paused. "Wait. Is this your one call from jail, or did you figure it out?"

"Jail? You called me," I answered with a snort.

She laughed and admitted I was right. "How are things?"

I sniffed. "The thing is, I might have figured it out, but I also might have just invited the murderer over to my house."

Frannie instantly chided me for letting too much of my Midwestern upbringing make my decisions. She insisted on calling the sheriff and hung up on me immediately. Ugh. She'd called the one person I didn't really want her to call.

So I ran into the grand entrance and came face-to-face with Sir Bogart strutting down the staircase. "You appear distressed, mistress."

My fingers laced together. "You think? Well, I'm pretty sure I figured out who murdered Gladys, but I also just invited said murderer to the house. And the sheriff will probably be on her way out here before long, too."

Bogey held none of the concerns of a human. He calmly sat down on the steps and cleaned his whiskers.

I peered up at him from the ground floor. "Bogey, did you hear what I said? I think Rodney killed Gladys, and I told him he could stop by and pick up his final payment. What should I do?"

Sir Bogart shrugged, and his velvety black fur glistened in the light. "Don't answer the door."

"But I talked to him on the phone two minutes ago. He knows I'm here."

The majestic cat sighed and strutted across the parquet floor. "How are your acting skills?"

Shrugging, I whispered, "I played a clown once in a junior high production."

Sir Bogart burst into his unique brand of laughter.

A cross between choking on a hairball and bones rattling in an attic. "Ah, thank you, mistress. Next to a new toy, or chasing a bit of string, that is a most glorious form of distraction. I did not intend for you to put on a performance for the masses. I would simply encourage you to play dumb. If you make no mention of the corpse in our mudroom, perhaps your transaction with Mr. Finley will come off without a hitch."

He had a point. It's not like Rodney was going to burst into my home and demand to search the place. If I acted like I had no idea, then maybe he'd do the same. That meant smiles and laughing and nothing at all serious, didn't it? I'd just hand over the check, make an excuse to explain my limited chatting, and also make no quick glances toward the mudroom. Just act normal, that's what it all boiled down to. That should be simple enough.

Gravel crunched under tires, alerting me that time was up.

I glanced at Bogey and shrugged. "Don't submit anything to the Academy yet."

Sir Bogart only blinked.

There was a firm knock at the front door, and I took a deep breath, shook my arms and shoulders, and pasted on a fake Fifth Avenue grin. "Hey,

Rodney. Wait right there. I'm gonna grab my checkbook."

I didn't want to raise suspicion by shutting the door in his face, but I also didn't want to invite him inside. We could conduct the transaction on the front porch. Thankfully, Rodney didn't put up a fight.

"Yes, ma'am," he answered through the door as I gently closed it between us.

I ran upstairs to the blue room to retrieve my purse and heard another vehicle approaching.

Suddenly, the front door of the manor slammed back open, and a shout echoed up from the first level. "You set me up, Sydney. I thought I could trust you."

Running to the banister, I looked down at an incredibly distraught Rodney in my foyer. Not only had he entered uninvited, but he'd also gone so pale even his lips had lost their color. Not good.

I scowled down at him from the second floor. "I don't know what you're talking about. I'm just grabbing my checkbook."

He shook his head and his hands balled into fists at his side. "What's the sheriff doing in your driveway, only seconds after I got here? Huh?"

Frannie. She'd sent Sheriff Allen right out. Cringing, I tried to figure out how to play it for Rodney's benefit. But before I could defend myself, my cell phone rang.

Rodney shouted up. "Don't answer that."

"Rodney, if I don't answer, it will be super suspicious."

He paced under the chandelier and shook his head. "Fine. Put it on speaker and don't say anything about me."

"Why would I, Rodney? You're only here picking up your payment." I couldn't tell if my attempt to call him down was working or not. Though, gauging by his pacing, I hadn't been successful at all.

I glanced at my phone, lowered the volume, and wondered if I could secretly signal Davis. Not that it was necessary, since apparently the sheriff was in my driveway. With all the sounds turned on, I couldn't text while I was on the phone either. Rodney would certainly hear the clicking of the keys.

My fake upbeat voice sounded hollow to my ears. "Hey, what's up?"

Davis ignored my unusually bubbly greeting. "Good news. I found that chandelier on my third phone call. The guy's eager to unload it, and he was willing to describe the salvager who dropped it off, for an extra five hundred on the price."

"Did you agree?" I turned away from the banister,

hating that I had to have this conversation on speaker phone. This would just send Rodney's suspicions into overdrive.

Sure enough, the shady handyman growled from the first floor. "Hurry up. Get off the phone."

Davis gave a self-satisfied sigh. "Of course. He described the guy as scrawny with dishwater blond hair and an unkempt mustache."

Glancing down at the scrawny, dishwater blond, with an unkempt mustache in my grand entrance, I gulped down a fresh lump of anxiety. "Oh. How interesting."

Rodney marched toward the steps, and the first one creaked beneath his slight weight. My chest tightened in fear as he climbed toward me.

Davis went on about something else, but I stopped listening.

"Thanks. I gotta go," I said. Then I shoved the phone into my pocket, and my hands shook as I tried to write out the check. "It's a hundred and fifty, right? I think that's how much I still owe you. Is that correct?"

The deep gong of the doorbell chimed, and Rodney's entire expression changed, darkened. "Sorry about this, Miss Coleman." He grabbed my arm, twisted it behind my back, and marched me down the stairs.

Struggling to hold back tears, I thought about my next move. Pain shot through my arm, into my shoulder, and threatened to make my knees buckle. The one that could keep me alive. I really didn't want to be the next ghost to haunt Moonlight Manor.

"Not that I don't trust you, Miss Coleman, but I'll be taking this." Rodney grabbed my phone from my pocket. Apparently, I hadn't locked the screen after the last call. He flipped through the call log. "What did Davis Martin want?"

"Oh, I needed something fixed in one of the bathrooms, and I just sent him a picture of the piece." Thankfully he hadn't managed to overhear Davis's side of the conversation despite it being on speaker phone. Unfortunately, my stupid made-up excuse sent Rodney directly to the photos on my phone. When he saw the wheelbarrow tracks, the mud on the step, and the tire tracks at the Williams estate, the jig was up.

My whimper nearly made it out, but I bit it back. Man, if I could've somehow forced the loop to reset right then, I certainly would've.

Rodney's mouth twisted into a hideous smile. "So you think you're pretty smart? You figured it all out and lured me here to serve me up to the sheriff." He deleted all the carefully collected evidence and laughed harshly. "There goes your case, Sherlock."

My lungs felt as though they were shrinking. This was the worst loop yet.

"You're just like everyone else. They're all out to get me. I'm only trying to make a living after that old biddy took everything from me. Why is everyone out to get me?"

"Maybe it's the stealing and the murdering." This smart-mouthed New Yorker would not go down without a fight. "Makes a difference, don't you think?"

The deep gonging of the doorbell came again.

Rodney leaned close and whispered menacingly, "You tell her everything's fine. But you're feeling real sick, and you don't want her to catch anything. Got it?"

"Got it."

He pushed me toward the door without releasing me, and I pressed my hand against the ancient wood. "Hello?" I called through the timbers.

"Miss Coleman? I need to come in," Sheriff Allen answered.

My throat hurt from holding back a flood of tears. "Hi, Sheriff, I'm super sick. I don't want you to catch what I have. It's been a terrible twenty-four hours." At least my voice sounded raspy enough to add credibility to the lie.

She knocked three times, and I flinched with each staccato report. "Miss Coleman. I received an anonymous tip reporting a murder on your property. It's probably a hoax, but I'm afraid I need you to open this door immediately."

Thank heaven for Frannie not listening to me. But I wasn't sure how to best take advantage of the Sheriff's arrival. Not with the thief and probable murderer right behind me.

Rodney wrenched my arm painfully, and I yelped without thinking.

A moment clicked by, and I held my breath. What would the sheriff do? What would *I* do?

"Is everything all right in there, Miss Coleman?"

Suddenly, everything happened at once.

Sir Bogart appeared, leapt through the air, and scratched mercilessly at Rodney's arm. Then he disappeared around the corner.

Rodney let go of me and swore a blue streak as I went spinning forward and away from him.

The sheriff forced the door open and nearly knocked me over.

Sadly, Rodney was quicker on his feet than he

looked. His expression turned stricken, and he turned frantic eyes to me. "Sheriff, Sheriff, I'm so glad you're here. She was gonna kill me, too."

What? What was he saying? My eyes shot wide open, and my jaw dangled. Useless in my time of need.

Sheriff Allen took a step back and drew her gun. "Who's the other victim?"

Rodney pretended to shake with fear. Or perhaps the attack of the ghost cat had genuinely frightened him. He raised a lonely index finger and pointed at me, and I had to admit he had enough acting chops that maybe he should get this year's Academy Award. "She— she killed Gladys Williams."

Finally, my vocal abilities returned. "I did no such thing," I snapped. "You killed Gladys Williams. And you were stealing stuff from her property and selling it on the black market. Then you murdered her and tossed her in my mudroom."

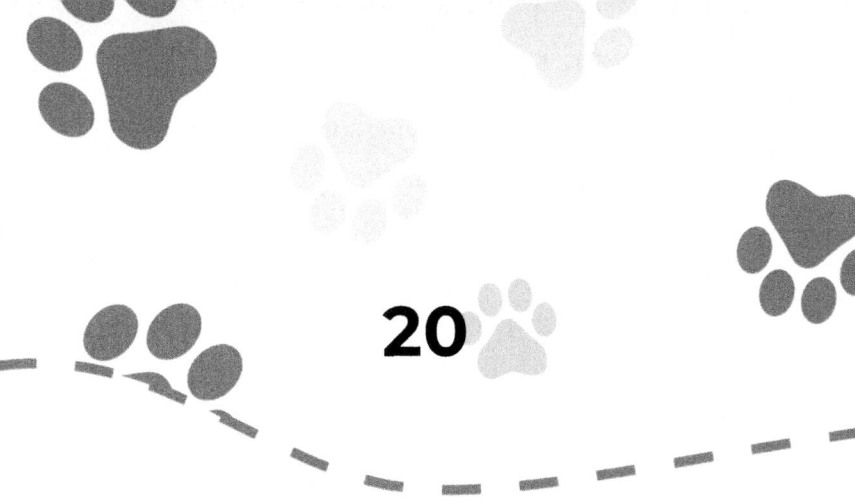

20

Sheriff Allen kept the gun trained on me, but there was a hint of doubt creeping into her blue eyes. "Is that true, Rodney?"

He glared at me, and something hard snapped in his eyes. "You gonna believe me or some murderer who just moved to town?"

A crack of thunder startled me into survival mode. "Look, Sheriff, I had evidence. I had pictures on my phone, but he took my phone and deleted the images. You can call Davis. He found one of the antique dealers that Rodney's been selling stuff to. And Gladys doesn't even live in her house anymore. She's living in a shack on my property." Oops, that last part was a bridge too far.

"Gladys Williams is living on your property?" Sheriff Allen tilted her head.

"Yes. I just found out yesterday—"

Rodney jumped in. "See. She had a run-in with Gladys yesterday, squatting illegally on her property, and today Gladys is dead. I had nothing to do with this sheriff. You know me. I keep to myself."

Sheriff Allen aimed her gun at a spot roughly between Rodney and me. It may seem like a small thing, but to me it meant the world. She had doubts, and I could work with doubt.

She called for backup and asked me for my phone.

I blew out a breath. "Sheriff, that's just it. I don't have my phone. Rodney has my phone because he was deleting the evidence."

She turned to the handyman. "Rodney, do you have Miss Coleman's phone?"

I'd seen a similar look of guilt settle on Lucas Aconite's face when I confronted his cheating butt. It looked very at home on Rodney's murdering mug, and I couldn't help the smug expression I knew I had.

From behind the right side of the imperial stairs, a ghostly cat eye peeked. Sir Bogart was still here, and I immediately felt safer. Surely, he could do something if everything went south.

"Come on, Rodney," Sheriff Allen prompted. "Do you have her phone?"

"It must've fallen out of her pocket. It's right here." He held the phone out toward Sheriff Allen. But I could sense every muscle in his body tensing like a cat about to pounce. The air practically snapped with tension.

Yet she didn't take the bait. "Slide it across the floor, Rodney."

He slid the phone, and when the sheriff bent to pick it up, he lunged at her. But he didn't get far. My big furry ghost hero used whatever otherworldly powers he possessed and sent Rodney hurtling backward into the wall. He slid down and landed on his stomach.

Go, Bogey. Go. I had to keep from cheering.

Rodney groaned and went limp.

A shocked Sheriff Allen looked at me and raised an eyebrow. "Sir Bogart?" she mouthed. She'd been friends with the ghost cat in the abandoned Moonlight Manor when she was a little girl and had still believed.

I nodded, smiled and tipped my head toward where the gloriously self-satisfied Sir Bogart sat.

Sheriff Allen glanced in the direction I'd indicated, but it was clear she still couldn't see him.

Haley mumbled her thanks under her breath. Then she grabbed Rodney's arms and for the first time in days and days, she clicked those blasted handcuffs around someone else's wrists.

The click of the cuffs closing brought Rodney around, and he bellowed a string of curse words. As Sheriff Allen pulled Rodney to his feet, he continued to profess his innocence and swore than he hadn't meant to smother Gladys. He tried to float some wild theory that she'd surprised him in the old Williams estate and he'd only covered her mouth to keep her from screaming.

Sheriff Allen jerked him roughly toward the door. "You can make an official statement at the station, Mr. Finley."

She walked him out of Moonlight Manor, down the stone stairs, and toward her car. He caterwauled the whole way, bellowing about his unfair life and how Gladys Williams had ruined his life.

As Sheriff Allen tucked the murderer in the back seat of her patrol car, I stopped on the threshold of my home, held my breath, and squeezed my eyes closed tight. Re-opening them as slowly as possible, I looked around to make sure I wasn't back in the attic. Then I stepped back inside the foyer and spun in a slow circle with my arms outstretched.

Success. Sir Bogart leapt onto the roundtable and put his paw on top of the crystal ball.

No reset. We did it.

Whatever the deeper meaning was behind that crazy spell I read from the grimoire, whether it was the justice of the ages or simply the justice Gladys Williams deserved, it had been served. Our tribulations were over . . .

Haley jogged back into the grand entrance to join me. "Miss Coleman, I'm sorry to have to do this. But I'll need you to cancel the tours for tonight. This is a crime scene now, and I can't have people traipsing through here until the investigation is closed."

You win some, you lose some. "I understand, Sheriff. I'll make the necessary phone calls, but maybe you don't have to mention Moonlight Manor in the report. The thing is, since the murder wasn't committed here, and tracks I found—"

Sheriff Allen had Rodney in the handcuffs in the backseat of her squad car, and she looked over her shoulder with sympathy in her eyes as she considered him. "Based on Rodney's story, it sounds like it happened next door, but an investigation like this is going to be the talk of the town. Regardless of the origin of the murder, the body ended up here. I'm afraid there's no way to keep Moonlight Manor out of the news. Sorry about all this."

Exhaling, I wiped a hand over my mouth and nodded. Haley waved, and the crunch of gravel beneath the sheriff's car filled the air. We'd solved another mystery and outed another murderer.

Once Sheriff Allen had exited the estate, I turned to the smug feline perched atop the grimoire and shrugged. "It looks like haunted tours aren't going to save us. Back to the drawing board, Sir Bogart."

I approached the sculpted walnut table with its eagle-talon feet and picked up the crystal ball. Gazing into its depths, I saw Frannie arriving. "Ya know what, Bogey? I think this thing is broken. Every time I look at it, the only thing I see is Frannie pulling into the driveway." I set the ball back on the display.

Sir Bogart swiped his paw across the polished surface, and a strange glow emanated from his golden eyes. "All magical orbs, like all spells, are not created equal. Each sphere must be cleansed and dedicated by its user. The crystal may be bathed in different herbal preparations and consecrated under a specific phase of the moon. In the end, it is the moonlight interacting with the herbal properties that imbues the ball with its abilities."

"All right. But—"

The front door flew open, and Frannie rushed toward me. She wrapped her comforting arms around me and exhaled loudly. "You did it. This whole thing has been absolutely insane. Time loops, repeating murders, you telling me not to call the sheriff."

As I hugged my best friend, the tears flowed. "It's okay, Frannie. I was so scared. I had no idea what Rodney was going to do. I'm so glad you didn't listen to me and called the sheriff anyway."

"I thought I saw that shady Rodney in the back of the cruiser as it went by." Frannie patted my back with kind, motherly affection, even though we were basically the same age. "So you're not angry? I know you kept telling me that no matter what, I shouldn't call Haley, but I got so worried."

Laughing through my tears, I squeezed her arm. "Trust me. I've never been so happy to have someone not listen to me in my entire life."

Distant sirens grew closer, and Frannie pressed a hand to her chest. "Is she still back there, in the mudroom?"

"Yeah. The sheriff said there'd be a crime scene team and whatever. I kind of want to get the body out of here." I sagged even as I said the words. As much as Gladys and I had never been friendly, she hadn't deserved to die by Rodney's hands. After her spending six months alone in the shack behind Moonlight Manor, I couldn't imagine she had been happy. It explained so much of her sourness and her stick-shaking.

The looping ordeal was over, but we had so much more to finish now. The investigation had to be completed, and the press would be clamoring for the story and commentary. And I knew I needed to attend Gladys's funeral when it was time. I wasn't sure how much of the community would attend, but I would.

Frannie squeezed my shoulder, drawing me out of the ramble of my thoughts. "As soon as you let them in, we'll head into town for a girl's day."

I grasped her hand and met her gaze, once again thankful for this unexpected friend who showed up when my world fell apart. "But, Frannie, don't you have to run the bakery? And I've got to call everyone who signed up for my tours and cancel their bookings tonight too."

She tilted her head and smirked. "You really don't get this business owner thing, do you? I'm in charge. I can close my bakery anytime I want. And if we split those calls between the two of us, we'll be done in no time. Then it's a full day of manicures, pedicures, maybe a facial . . . Whatever we want." She leaned close and lowered her voice. "I think breaking out of the time loop-de-loop that was your life is reason enough to treat ourselves, don't you?"

"You have a point." I glanced at the crystal ball, and my eyes slowly slipped toward Sir Bogart. "You know what, Bogey. Whatever herbs and moon phases were used, I think that crystal ball is only meant to deliver good news."

Frannie looked at the empty space on the display table and shrugged. "Hello to the Bogey-cat."

Bogey flinched. "I do not give her permission to call me by anything other than Sir Bogart."

I shrugged. "You can work it out with her next time she sees you."

Bogey winked slyly in my direction before he vanished. The vehicles— and, yes, that is plural— were circling the fountain. They killed the sirens but left the lights flashing.

I caught her elbow. "Hey, I hate to ask, but can you do me one more favor?"

Frannie nodded, and her red curls bounced with the movement of her head. "Of course. Name it."

I jerked my thumb toward the grimoire. "I need to get that incredibly dangerous book back up to the attic. It's not a prop or a book of poems, in case you were wondering. So can you let the deputies in?"

She glanced at the book, and I saw the goosebumps rise on her forearms. "Creepy. But yeah, I've got you. Do whatever you need to do."

I grabbed the book and the orb. Hurrying up the steps, I left the good news globe, as I planned to call it, in the blue room in the middle of my bed until I could find a holder for it and returned the grimoire to its rightful place in the attic. Slamming the lid of the trunk, a weight slid from my shoulders.

Maybe, with Sir Bogart's guidance, I could explore the Blodfyss sisters' grimoire with more patience and care . . . and no repeating of any of the poems. I'd already learned a couple of lessons in this manor. The first was not to take anything I discovered lightly, and the second was that I really could rely on myself. I was pretty okay, exactly as I was.

New York now seemed like another lifetime, and frankly, that was all right with me.

An unwelcome visitor. A surprising past. Will her fire sale go up in smoke?

CLICK HERE to get your copy of *Moonlight and Mayhem,* so that you can keep reading this series today!

WHAT'S NEXT?

Sydney Coleman has one last chance to save her manor, and to do it, she'll have to sell off some precious heirlooms she found stashed in the attic. Of course, her plans go topsy turvy when her vindictive ex shows up!

The auction turns into a bidding war, and Sydney worries there'll be actual casualties. She tries to smooth things over, but when her old boyfriend winds up dead—she's the number one suspect.

Can Sydney sift through the confusing clues and find the killer, or are all sales final?

What happens next?
Don't wait to find out...

MOONLIGHT AND MAYHEM is now available.

Purchase your copy so that you can keep reading this zany mystery series today!

SNEAK PEEK
MOONLIGHT & MAYHEM

Third time's the charm. I'd heard that saying many times while growing up but never felt the weight of its scope until now. After my unceremonious exit from New York City, I began to rebuild my life in Misty Meadows. Somehow, after stumbling upon the deal of the century, I'd purchased a Gothic mansion called Moonlight Manor.

At the time of purchase, I hadn't known about the trio of residents I inherited when declaring myself mistress of the mansion. Hindsight being what it was, I doubted if knowing about them would have stopped me from making the manor my home. The place offered a fresh start I needed with a price tag that made it possible.

My realtor, Mia, had touted its nineteenth century

beauty. "The exterior is clad in rusticated granite and the front elevation is composed of two distinct towers. The one on the right is cylindrical and adds a little bump-out to the first floor drawing room and second floor main suite. The top of that round tower is trimmed with what's called egg-and-dart molding and capped by a conical Tyrolean roof. Technically, that's more of a Scottish Baronial feature, but because the home was built during the Gothic Revival period, it's still classified as Gothic."

Although, it wasn't until I ventured into the mysterious attic, hidden behind a solid door with an antique glass knob, that I fell in love with the place. Of course, loving it wasn't enough. I had to figure out how to make some money if I wanted to continue living with my three *ghostly* roommates. At least if I wanted to keep the lights on and continue eating. Not that my new friends cared much about either of those things.

Yet I didn't give up easily, and I had a head full of fabulous ideas.

Attempt number one had been a bed-and-breakfast, but after one of the most influential travel editors in the eastern United States skewered my property in a scathing review, that adventure crumbled. The travel editor didn't appreciate the nightmares and apparitions caused by the previous mistress of the manor being trapped between here and the hereafter.

Not to worry, my roots are solid, Midwestern stock. So I picked myself up and figuratively brushed the manure off—as I had literally done so many times on my father's pig farm. I'd learned the only thing between me and success was time and hard work, right? After we freed Beatrix de Haviland from her disquiet, she passed through to her final rest, and we were able to move on as well.

So I came up with idea number two in month number two. Since I shared my residence with three enterprising apparitions, two human and one feline, I opted to lean into the theme that presented itself. I set up haunted mansion tours for All Hallows Eve, and using my online marketing expertise, pretty much sold out for the season in four days.

Velma, Norman, and Sir Bogart, the beloved feline pet of Miss de Haviland, helped turn haunted Moonlight Manor into a thrill to behold. We were positioned to receive rave reviews for a new and blossoming business.

Unfortunately, on opening weekend, a real live—well, let me rephrase—an actual corpse turned up in my mudroom. So, that was Plan B down the toilet.

Here I am, once again brushing the dust from my hands and dungarees. All I needed now was an amazing Plan C.

Yes, this was most definitely a case of getting the girl out of Iowa but being unable to get the Iowa out of the girl.

I remained bullish, determined. Giving up, throwing in the towel, calling it quits? No way. Nuh-uh. Not going to happen.

We'd figure out a lucrative, workable idea. I was sure of it. Though, it would probably take all four of us to do so.

Seated nearby, the self-appointed Lord of the Manor, His Royal Felineness, Bogart the First, the Only, the Eternal, was a wealth of information. He'd been the best friend to a wealthy and influential costume designer during the Golden Age of film. He literally rubbed shoulders with some of the wealthiest families on the eastern seaboard, and in his ensuing years as a ghost, had accumulated knowledge in the areas of magic, manors, and antiques.

In the center of the drawing room, I hugged my mug of Velma's special tea to my chest to fend off the stress-ache forming there. "Sir Bogart, I was wondering if you could help me come up with a new plan to keep us afloat?"

His silky black fur glistened from within as he curled onto an ottoman and asked—no, *demanded*—to be placed in front of the fireplace in the drawing room. The winter wind sighed around the outside of the tower.

"Does the fire actually warm you?" I stared at the flickering flames, visible through his translucent body. The way the light refracted through his vaporous form mesmerized me.

He stretched lazily. "No, mistress. Although, the memory of such things keeps me from going mad."

His words reminded me of Velma's vicarious enjoyment when I described eating a caramel-apple cupcake to her. It had made her sad to be reminded of what she couldn't experience, but she had closed her eyes and tried to remember.

I took a sip of my tea and savored the mouth feel before I swallowed. Existing as a physical being did have its benefits. "I thought perhaps for our next venture, we could try something with antiques. I've learned a lot since purchasing the manor, and you seem to be a bottomless well of information on the subject."

He ignored my question and my flattery.

"Bogey, did you not hear me, or are you choosing not to answer?"

He rested his majestic head on a paw and stared at me with his all-knowing yellow eyes. "I heard you, mistress. However, I was pondering the wisdom of purchasing antiques, as you call them, to sell when you own a mansion full of them."

He had a point. "What are you suggesting?" I took another sip.

"Perhaps you, myself, cook, and butler could inventory the contents of the manor. There are certain things that will have sentimental value to the three of us who lived and died within these walls. However, I'm certain there will be a multitude of items which would fetch a handsome price if you were to locate suitable buyers."

For a moment, I forgot the brilliant feline was a ghost and attempted to stroke his back. My fingers drifted through his energy, but despite his lack of corporeal form, he seemed to purr.

"Can you feel that?" I asked, repeating the action.

"Once again, it is the memory—however distant—that brings me comfort."

Despite the slight twist in my chest from his words, I continued. "Well, I think you've had a wonderful idea. I'm going to run into town for supplies. Would you like a new toy while I'm out?"

His wide, glowing eyes closed to slits, and the nod of his head was nearly imperceptible.

When I'd arrived, mere months ago, his worn and tattered toys littered the attic. But in exchange for new and exciting forms of entertainment, we'd reached a détente. He offered advice, whether or not I asked for it, and I fetched him the occasional feathered plaything.

He closed his eyes all the way and remained stationary on the ottoman. "In your absence, I shall discuss the plan with Velma and Norman."

"Thanks. I'll be back in an hour or so. I'll probably stop at Heaven Can Bake and enjoy a coffee and some gossip with Frannie."

His eyes remained closed, but he hummed in agreement. "Safe journeys, mistress."

MOONLIGHT AND MAYHEM is now available.

Purchase your copy so that you can keep reading this zany mystery series today!

ABOUT TRIXIE SILVERTALE

Trixie Silvertale grew up reading an endless supply of Lilian Jackson Braun, Hardy Boys, and Nancy Drew novels. She loves the amateur sleuths in cozy mysteries and obsesses about all things paranormal. Those two passions unite in her paranormal cozy mystery series, and she's thrilled to write them and share them with you.

When she's not consumed by writing, she bakes to fuel her creative engine and pulls weeds in her herb garden to clear her head (*and sometimes she pulls out her hair, but mostly weeds*).

If you're looking for more from Trixie Silvertale, sign up for her monthly newsletter at **trixiesilvertale.com/paranormal-cozy-club-2/**

Greetings are welcome:
trixie@trixiesilvertale.com
Bookbub | Facebook | Instagram

Click here to **Join Trixie's Club!**

A NOTE FROM TRIXIE

I've always been a huge fan of haunted mansions . . .

The best part of "living" in Misty Meadows was the chance to build a brand new world, and meet Sydney Coleman and Sir Bogart. And big "spooky" hugs to the world's best ARC Team – Trixie's Mystery ARC Detectives!

It was an honor and a pleasure to work with Molly Fitz and Whiskered Mysteries. They offered me the opportunity to step into a wonderful new tale, for a book or three, and I loved it.

I'm especially grateful for the helpful architecture info provided by Michael. Thanks to Josh and Morgan for making me watch scary movies!

FUN FACT: One of my favorite movies is *Groundhog Day*.

SECRET: I've never written a time-loop mystery, but I always wanted to! Thanks for letting me check something off my Bucket List. It was such a challenging and exciting experience.

I hope you'll continue to explore the mansion with us.

TRIXIE SILVERTALE (SEPTEMBER 2022)

MITZY MOON MYSTERIES

A gift that's too good to be true. A murder she didn't commit. A barista in a latte trouble…

Mitzy Moon believes she's an orphan, so she's dumbstruck when a special delivery to her low-rent apartment reveals a family. But her shock turns to awe when she discovers her grandmother left her a fortune, a fiendish feline, and a bookshop of rare tomes brimming with magic. Start with Book 1: **Fries and Alibis**.

MAGICAL RENAISSANCE FAIRE MYSTERIES

A dubious festival. A fatal swim. Can this fortune-telling fairy herald the true killer?

Coriander the Conjurer is trapped in a cursed Renaissance Faire, but that's the good news. Her usual routine of reading patrons' futures and compensating for her lopsided fairy wings is interrupted when a scuffle turns deadly. Now, in order to broker peace within the realm she must solve a mermaid's murder. But she'll need the help of a dangerous vampire and her meddling toad familiar to uncover the real clues. Start the adventure with **All Swell That Ends Spell.**

ABOUT MOLLY FITZ

While *USA Today bestselling* author Molly Fitz can't technically talk to animals, she and her three feline writing assistants have deep and very animated conversations as they navigate their days.

She lives with her husband, child, and their own private zoo somewhere in the wilds of Alaska. Molly will occasionally venture out for good food, great coffee, or to meet new animal friends.

Learn more about Molly and her books, and be sure to sign up for her newsletter at **www.MollyMysteries.com**.

ALSO BY MOLLY FITZ

Learn more about Molly's collected works, so that you can decide which book you'd like to read next...

PET WHISPERER P.I.

Angie Russo just partnered up with Blueberry Bay's first ever talking cat detective. Along with his ragtag gang of human and animal helpers, Octo-Cat is determined to save the day... so long as it doesn't interfere with his schedule.

Start with book 1, ***Kitty Confidential***.

MERLIN'S MAGICAL MYSTERIES

Gracie Springs is not a witch... but her cat is. Now she must help to keep his secret or risk spending the rest of her life in some magical prison. Too bad trouble seems to find them at every turn!

Start with book 1, ***Merlin Takes a Familiar***.

PARANORMAL TEMP AGENCY

Tawny Bigford's simple life takes a turn for the magical when she stumbles upon her landlady's murder and is recruited by a talking black cat named Fluffikins to take over the deceased's role as the official Town Witch for Beech Grove, Georgia.

Start with book 1, ***Witch for Hire***.

THE MYSTERIES OF MOONLIGHT MANOR (WITH TRIXIE SILVERTALE)

Sydney Coleman has it all—until she doesn't. No sooner does she launch her bed and breakfast, than a trio of ghosts turn up oppose her at every turn. They insist she solve the murder of their mistress, but Sydney is desperate for cash. If she can't book some guests fast, her haunted mansion is utterly doomed.

Start with book 1, ***Moonlight & Mischief.***

CONNECT WITH MOLLY

Sign up for my newsletter and get a special digital prize pack for joining, including an exclusive story, *Meowy Christmas Mayhem*, fun quiz, and lots of cat pictures!

Sign up: **MollyMysteries.com/subscribe**

Now, if you ever wished you could converse with cats, here's your opportunity! This is me officially inviting you into my whacky inner world as part of my Cozy Kitty Book Club.

For those who just can't get enough of my zany cat characters and their hapless humans, this book club will provide new content to devour and the chance to get to know my best author friends.

From exclusive stories, behind-the-scenes trivia to never-before-released bonus content, and monthly giveaways, there's a lot to love about the Cozy Kitty

Book Club. Join today to find out what we're reading next!

Join: **MollyMysteries.com/club**

Printed in Dunstable, United Kingdom